I0642209

Charles Dudley Warner

As we were saying

With illustrations

Charles Dudley Warner

As we were saying
With illustrations

ISBN/EAN: 9783743303515

Manufactured in Europe, USA, Canada, Australia, Japa

Cover: Foto ©Andreas Hilbeck / pixelio.de

Manufactured and distributed by brebook publishing software
(www.brebook.com)

Charles Dudley Warner

As we were saying

AS WE WERE SAYING

BY CHAS. DUDLEY WARNER

WITH ILLUSTRATIONS BY HARRY
WHITNEY McVICKAR, AND OTHERS
PUBLISHED BY . . . .

HARPER & BROTHERS

NEW YORK   MDCCCXCI

. . . .

Copyright, 1891, by HARPER & BROTHERS

———

All rights reserved

CONTENTS.

ROSE AND CHRYSANTHEMUM.

HE Drawer will still bet on the rose. This is not a wager, but only a strong expression of opinion. The rose will win. It does not look so now. To all appearances, this is the age of the chrysanthemum. What this gaudy flower will be, daily expanding and varying to suit the whim of fashion, no one can tell. It may be made to bloom like the cabbage; it may spread out like an umbrella—it can never be large enough nor showy enough to suit us. Undeniably it is very effective, especially in masses of gorgeous color. In its innumerable shades and enlarging proportions, it is a triumph of the gardener. It is a rival to the aniline dyes and to the marabout feathers. It goes along with all the conceits and fantastic unrest of the decorative art. Indeed, but for the discovery of the capacities of the chrysanthemum, modern life would have experienced a fatal hitch in its development. It helps out our age of plush with a flame of color. There is nothing shamefaced or retiring about it, and it already takes all provinces for its own. One would be only half married—civilly, and not fashionably—without a chrysanthemum wedding; and it lights the way to the tomb. The maiden wears a bunch of it in her corsage in token of her blooming expectations, and the young man flaunts it on his coat lapel in an effort to be at once effective and in the mode. Young love that used to express its timid desire with the violet, or, in its ardor, with the carnation, now seeks to bring its emotions to light by the help of the chrysanthemum. And it can express every shade of feeling, from the rich yellow of prosperous wooing to the brick-colored weariness of life that is hardly distinguishable from the liver complaint. It is a little stringy for a boutonnière, but it fills the modern-trained eye as no other flower can fill it. We used to say that a girl was as sweet as a rose; we have forgotten that language. We used to call those tender additions to society, on the eve of their advent into that world which is always so eager to receive fresh young life, "rose-buds;" we say now simply "buds," but we mean chrysanthemum buds. They are as beautiful as ever; they excite the same exquisite interest; perhaps in their maiden hearts they are one or another variety of that flower which bears such a sweet perfume in all literature; but can it make no difference in character whether a young girl comes out into the garish world as a rose or as a chrysanthemum? Is her life set to the note of display, of color and show, with little sweetness, or to that retiring modesty which needs a little encouragement before it fully reveals its beauty and its perfume? If one were to pass his life in moving in a palace car from one plush hotel to another, a bunch of chrysanthemums in his hand would seem to be a good symbol of his life. There are aged people who can remember that they used to choose various roses, as to their color, odor, and degree of unfolding, to express the delicate shades of advancing passion and of devotion. What can one do with this new favorite? Is not a bunch of chrysanthemums a sort of take-it-or-leave-it declaration, boldly and showily made, an offer without discrimination, a tender without romance? A young man will catch the whole family with this flaming message, but where is that sentiment that once set the maiden heart in a flutter? Will she press a chrysanthemum, and keep it till the faint perfume reminds her of the sweetest moment of her life?

Are we exaggerating this astonishing rise, development, and spread of the chrysanthemum? As a fashion it is not so extraordinary as the hoop-skirt, or as the neck ruff, which is again rising as a background to the lovely head. But the remarkable thing about it is that heretofore in all nations and times, and in all changes of fashion in dress, the rose has held its own as the queen of flowers and as the finest expression of sentiment. But here comes a flaunting thing with no desirable perfume, looking as if it were cut with scissors out of tissue-paper, but capable of taking infinite varieties of color, and growing as big as a curtain tassel, that literally captures the world, and spreads all over the globe, like the Canada thistle. The florists have no eye for anything else, and the biggest floral prizes are awarded for the production of its eccentricities. Is the rage for this flower typical of this fast and flaring age?

The Drawer is not an enemy to the chrysanthemum, nor to the sunflower, nor to any other gorgeous production of nature. But it has an old-fashioned love for the modest and unobtrusive virtues, and an abiding faith that they will win over the strained and strident displays of life. There is the violet: all efforts of cultivation fail to make it as big as the peony, and it would be no more dear to the heart if it were quadrupled in size. We do, indeed, know that satisfying beauty and refinement are apt to escape us when we strive too much and force nature into extraordinary display, and we know how difficult it is to get mere bigness and show without vulgarity. Cultivation has its limits. After we have produced it, we find that the biggest rose even is not the most precious; and lovely as woman is, we instinctively in our admiration put a limit to her size. There being, then, certain laws that ultimately fetch us all up standing, so to speak, it does seem probable that the chrysanthemum rage will end in a gorgeous sunset of its splendor; that fashion will tire of it, and that the rose, with its secret heart of love; the rose, with its exquisite form; the rose, with its capacity of shyly and reluctantly unfolding its beauty; the rose, with that odor—of the first garden exhaled and yet kept down through all the ages of sin—will become again the fashion, and be more passionately admired for its temporary banishment. Perhaps the poet will then come back again and sing. What poet could now sing of the "awful chrysanthemum of dawn?"

THE RED BONNET.

HE Drawer has no wish to make Lent easier for anybody, or rather to diminish the benefit of the penitential season. But in this period of human anxiety and repentance it must be said that not enough account is made of the moral responsibility of Things. The doctrine is sound; the only difficulty is in applying it. It can, however, be illustrated by a little story, which is here confided to the reader in the same trust in which it was received. There was once a lady, sober in mind and sedate in manner, whose plain dress exactly represented her desire to be inconspicuous, to do good, to improve every day of her life in actions that should benefit her kind. She was a serious person, inclined to improving conversation, to the reading of bound books that cost at least a dollar and a half (fifteen cents of which she gladly contributed to the author), and she had a distaste for the gay society which was mainly a flutter of ribbons and talk and pretty faces; and when she meditated, as she did in her spare moments, her heart was sore over the frivolity of life and the emptiness of fashion. She longed to make the world better, and without any priggishness she set it an example of simplicity and sobriety, of cheerful acquiescence in plainness and inconspicuousness.

One day—it was in the autumn—this lady had occasion to buy a new hat. From a great number offered to her she selected a red one with a dull red plume. It did not agree with the rest of her apparel; it did not fit her apparent character. What impulse led to this selection she could not explain. She was not tired of being good, but something in the jauntiness of the hat and the color pleased her. If it were a temptation, she did not intend to yield to it, but she thought she would take the hat home and try it. Perhaps her nature felt the need of a little warmth. The hat pleased her still more when she got it home and put it on and surveyed herself in the mirror. Indeed, there was a new expression in her face that corresponded to the hat. She put it off and looked at it. There was something almost humanly winning and temptatious in it. In short, she kept it, and when she wore it abroad she was not conscious of its incongruity to herself or to her dress, but of the incongruity of the rest of her apparel to the hat, which seemed to have a sort of intelligence of its own, at least a power of changing and conforming things to itself. By degrees one article after another in the lady's wardrobe was laid aside, and another substituted for it that answered to the demanding spirit of the hat. In a little while this plain lady was not plain any more, but most gorgeously dressed, and possessed with the desire to be in the height of the fashion. It came to this, that she had a tea gown made out of a window-curtain with a flamboyant pattern. Solomon in all his glory would have been ashamed of himself in her presence.

But this was not all. Her disposition, her ideas, her whole life, were changed. She did not any more think of going about doing good, but of amusing herself. She read nothing but stories in paper covers. In place of being sedate and sober-minded, she was frivolous to excess; she spent most of her time with women who liked to " frivol." She kept Lent in the most expensive way, so as to make the impression upon everybody that she was better than the extremest kind of Lent. From liking the sedatest company she passed to liking the gayest society and the most fashionable method of getting rid of her time. Nothing whatever bad happened to her, and she is now an ornament to society.

This story is not an invention; it is a leaf out of life. If this lady that autumn day had bought a plain bonnet she would have continued on in her humble, sensible way of living. Clearly it was the hat that made the woman, and not the woman the hat. She had no preconception of it; it simply happened to her, like any accident —as if she had fallen and sprained her ankle. Some people may say that she had in her a concealed propensity for frivolity; but the hat cannot escape the moral responsibility of calling it out if it really existed. The power of things to change and create character is well attested. Men live up to or live down to their clothes, which have a great moral influence on manner, and even on conduct. There was a man run down almost to vagabondage, owing to his increasingly shabby clothing, and he was only saved from becoming a moral and physical wreck by a remnant of good - breeding in him that kept his worn boots well polished. In time his boots brought up the rest of his apparel and set him on his feet again. Then there is the well-known example of the honest clerk on a small salary who was ruined by the gift of a repeating watch—an expensive time-piece that required at least ten thousand a year to sustain it: he is now in Canada.

Sometimes the influence of Things is good and sometimes it is bad. We need a philosophy that shall tell us why it is one or the other, and fix the responsibility where it belongs. It does no good, as people always find out by reflex action, to kick an inanimate thing that has offended, to smash a perverse watch with a hammer, to break a rocking-chair that has a habit of tipping over backward. If Things are not actually malicious, they seem to have a power of revenging themselves. We ought to try to understand them better, and to be more aware of what they can do to us. If the lady who bought the red hat could have known the hidden nature of it, could have had a vision of herself as she was transformed by it, she would as soon have taken a viper into her bosom as have placed the red tempter on her head. Her whole previous life, her feeling of the moment, show that it was not vanity that changed her, but the inconsiderate association with a Thing that happened to strike her fancy, and which seemed innocent. But no Thing is really powerless for good or evil.

THE LOSS IN CIVILIZATION.

HAVE we yet hit upon the right idea of civilization? The process which has been going on ever since the world began seems to have a defect in it; strength, vital power, somehow escapes. When you've got a man thoroughly civilized you cannot do anything more with him. And it is worth reflection what we should do, what could we spend our energies on, and what would

evoke them, we who are both civilized
and enlightened, if all nations were civilized and the earth were entirely subdued. That is to say, are not barbarism
and vast regions of uncultivated land a
necessity of healthful life on this globe?
We do not like to admit that this process
has its cycles, that nations and men, like
trees and fruit, grow, ripen, and then de-
cay. The world has always had a conceit that the globe could be made entirely habitable, and all over the home of a
society constantly growing better. In order to accomplish this we have striven to
eliminate barbarism in man and in nature.

Is there anything more unsatisfactory
than a perfect house, perfect grounds,
perfect gardens, art and nature brought
into the most absolute harmony of taste
and culture? What more can a man do
with it? What satisfaction has a man in
it if he really gets to the end of his power
to improve it? There have been such
nearly ideal places, and how strong nature, always working against man and in
the interest of untamed wildness, likes to
riot in them and reduce them to pictu-

resque destruction! And what sweet sad-
ness, pathos, romantic suggestion, the
human mind finds in such a ruin! And
a society that has attained its end in all
possible culture, entire refinement in manners, in tastes, in the art of elegant intellectual and luxurious living — is there
nothing pathetic in that? Where is the
primeval, heroic force that made the joy
of living in the rough old uncivilized
days? Even throw in goodness, a certain amount of altruism, gentleness, warm
interest in unfortunate humanity—is the
situation much improved? London is
probably the most civilized centre the
world has ever seen; there are gathered
more of the elements of that which we
reckon the best. Where in history, unless
some one puts in a claim for the French-
man, shall we find a Man so nearly approaching the standard we have set up
of civilization as the Englishman, refined
by inheritance and tradition, educated
almost beyond the disturbance of enthu-
siasm, and cultivated beyond the chance
of surprise? We are speaking of the highest type in manner, information, training,

in the acquisition of what the world has to give. Could these men have conquered the world? Is it possible that our highest civilization has lost something of the rough and admirable element that we admire in the heroes of Homer and of Elizabeth? What is this London, the most civilized city ever known? Why, a considerable part of its population is more barbarous, more hopelessly barbarous, than any wild race we know, because they are the barbarians of civilization, the refuse and slag of it, if we dare say that of any humanity. More hopeless, because the virility of savagery has measurably gone out of it. We can do something with a degraded race of savages, if it has any stamina in it. What can be done with those who are described as " East-Londoners ?"

Every great city has enough of the same element. Is this an accident, or is it a necessity of the refinement that we insist on calling civilization? We are always sending out missionaries to savage or perverted nations, we are always sending out emigrants to occupy and reduce to order neglected territory. This is our main business. How would it be if this business were really accomplished, and there were no more peoples to teach our way of life to, and no more territory to bring under productive cultivation? Without the necessity of putting forth this energy, a survival of the original force in man, how long would our civilization last? In a word, if the world were actually all civilized, wouldn't it be too weak even to ripen? And now, in the great centres, where is accumulated most of that we value as the product of man's best efforts, is there strength enough to elevate the degraded humanity that attends our highest cultivation? We have a gay confidence that we can do something for Africa. Can we reform London and Paris and New York, which our own hands have made?

If we cannot, where is the difficulty? Is this a hopeless world? Must it always go on by spurts and relapses, alternate civilization and barbarism, and the barbarism being necessary to keep us employed and growing? Or is there some mistake about our ideal of civilization? Does our process too much eliminate the rough vigor, courage, stamina of the race? After a time do we just live, or try to live, on literature warmed over, on pretty coloring and drawing instead of painting that stirs the soul to the heroic facts and tragedies of life? Where did this virile, blood-full, throbbing Russian literature come from; this Russian painting of Verestchagin, that smites us like a sword with the consciousness of the tremendous meaning of existence? Is there a barbaric force left in the world that we have been daintily trying to cover and apologize for and refine into gentle agreeableness?

These questions are too deep for these pages. Let us make the world pleasant, and throw a cover over the refuse. We are doing very well, on the whole, considering what we are and the materials we have to work on. And we must not leave the world so perfectly civilized that the inhabitants, two or three centuries ahead, will have nothing to do.

SOCIAL SCREAMING.

OF all the contrivances for amusement in this agreeable world the "Reception" is the most ingenious, and would probably most excite the wonder of an angel sent down to inspect our social life. If he should pause at the entrance of the house where one is in progress, he would be puzzled. The noise that would greet his ears is different from the deep continuous roar in the streets, it is unlike the hum of millions of seventeen-year locusts, it wants the musical quality of the spring conventions of the blackbirds in the chestnuts, and he could not compare it to the vociferation in a lunatic asylum, for that is really subdued and infrequent. He might be incapable of analyzing this, but when he caught sight of the company he would be compelled to recognize it as the noise of our highest civilization. It may not be perfect, for there are limits to human powers of endurance, but it is the best we can do. It is not a chance affair. Here are selected, picked out by special invitation, the best that society can show, the most intelligent, the most accomplished, the most beautiful, the best dressed persons in the community — all receptions have this character. The angel would notice this at once, and he would be astonished at the number of such persons, for the rooms would be so crowded that he would see the hopelessness of attempting to edge or wedge his way through the throng without tearing off his wings. An angel, in short, would stand no chance in one of these brilliant assemblies on account of his wings, and he probably could not be heard, on account of the low, heavenly pitch of his voice. His inference would be that these people had been selected to come together by reason of their superior power of screaming. He would be wrong. They are selected on account of their intelligence, agreeableness, and power of entertaining each other. They come together, not for exercise, but pleasure, and the more they crowd and jam and struggle, and the louder they scream, the greater the pleasure. It is a kind of contest, full of good - humor and excitement. The one that has the shrillest voice and can scream the loudest is most successful. It would seem at first that they are under a singular hallucination, imagining that the more noise there is in the room the better each one can be heard, and so each one continues to raise his or her voice in order to drown the other voices. The secret of the game is to pitch the voice one or two octaves above the ordinary tone. Some throats cannot stand this strain long ; they become rasped and sore, and the voices break ; but this adds to the excitement and enjoyment of those who can scream with less inconvenience. The angel would notice that if at any time silence was called, in order that an announcement of music could be made, in the awful hush that followed people spoke to each other in their natural voices, and everybody could be heard without effort. But this was not the object of the Reception, and in a moment more the screaming would begin again, the voices growing higher and higher, until, if the roof were taken off, one vast shriek would go up to heaven.

This is not only a fashion, it is an art. People have to train for it, and as it is a unique amusement, it is worth some trouble to be able to succeed in it. Men, by reason of their stolidity and deeper voices, can never be proficients in it; and they do not have so much practice—unless they are stock-brokers. Ladies keep themselves in training in their ordinary calls. If three or four meet in a drawing-room they all begin to scream, not that they may be heard—for the higher they go the less they understand each other—but simply to acquire the art of screaming at receptions. If half a dozen ladies meeting by chance in a parlor should converse quietly in their sweet, ordinary home tones, it might be in a certain sense agreeable, but it would not be fashionable, and it would not strike the prevailing note of our civilization. If it were true that a group of women all like to talk at the same time when they meet (which is a slander invented by men, who may be just as loquacious, but not so limber-tongued and quick-witted), and raise their voices to a shriek in order to dominate each other, it could be demonstrated that they would be more readily heard if they all spoke in low tones. But the object is not conversation; it is the social exhilaration that comes from the wild exercise of the voice in working off a nervous energy; it is so seldom that in her own house a lady gets a chance to scream.

The dinner-party, where there are ten or twelve at table, is a favorite chance for this exercise. At a recent dinner, where there were a dozen uncommonly intelligent people, all capable of the most entertaining conversation, by some chance, or owing to some nervous condition, they all began to speak in a high voice as soon as they were seated, and the effect was that of a dynamite explosion. It was a cheerful babel of indistinguishable noise, so loud and shrill and continuous that it was absolutely impossible for two people seated on the opposite sides of the table, and both shouting at each other, to catch an intelligible sentence. This made a lively dinner. Everybody was animated, and if there was no conversation, even between persons seated side by side, there was a glorious clatter and roar; and when it was over, everybody was hoarse and exhausted, and conscious that he had done his best in a high social function.

This topic is not the selection of the Drawer, the province of which is to note, but not to criticise, the higher civilization. But the inquiry has come from many cities, from many women, "Cannot something be done to stop social screaming?" The question is referred to the scientific branch of the Social Science Association. If it is a mere fashion, the association can do nothing. But it might institute some practical experiments. It might get together in a small room fifty people all let loose in the ordinary screaming contest, measure the total volume of noise and divide it by fifty, and ascertain how much throat power was needed in one person to be audible to another three feet from the latter's ear. This would sift out the persons fit for such a contest. The investigator might then call a dead silence in the assembly, and request each person to talk in a natural voice, then divide the total noise as before, and see what chance of being heard an ordinary individual had in it. If it turned out in these circumstances that every person present could speak with ease and hear perfectly what was said, then the order might be given for the talk to go on in that tone, and that every person who raised the voice and began to scream should be gagged and removed to another room. In this room could be collected all the screamers to enjoy their own powers. The same experiment might be tried at a dinner-party, namely, to ascertain if the total hum of low voices in the natural key would not be less for the individual voice to overcome than the total scream of all the voices raised to a shriek. If scientific research demonstrated the feasibility of speaking in an ordinary voice at receptions, dinner-parties, and in "calls," then the Drawer is of opinion that intelligible and enjoyable conversation would be possible on these occasions, if it becomes fashionable not to scream.

DOES REFINEMENT KILL
INDIVIDUALITY?

S it true that cultivation, what we call
refinement, kills individuality? Or,
worse than that even, that one loses his
taste by overcultivation? Those persons
are uninteresting, certainly, who have gone
so far in culture that they accept conventional standards supposed to be correct, to which they refer everything, and
by which they measure everybody. Taste
usually implies a sort of selection; the
cultivated taste of which we speak is merely a comparison, no longer an individual
preference or appreciation, but only a re-
ference to the conventional and accepted
standard. When a man or woman has
reached this stage of propriety we are
never curious any more concerning their

opinions on any subject. We know that
the opinions expressed will not be theirs,
evolved out of their own feeling, but that
they will be the cut-and-dried results of
conventionality.

It is doubtless a great comfort to a person to know exactly how to feel and what
to say in every new contingency, but
whether the zest of life is not dulled by
this ability is a grave question, for it leaves
no room for surprise and little for emotion. O ye belles of Newport and of Bar
Harbor, in your correct and conventional
agreement of what is proper and agreeable, are you wasting your sweet lives by
rule? Is your compact, graceful, orderly
society liable to be monotonous in its
gay repetition of the same thing week
after week? Is there nothing outside of
that envied circle which you make so
brilliant? Is the Atlantic shore the only
coast where beauty may lounge and spread
its net of enchantment? The Atlantic
shore and Europe? Perhaps on the Pa-
cific you might come back to your original selves, and find again that freedom
and that charm of individuality that are

so attractive. Some sparkling summer morning, if you chanced to drive four-in-hand along the broad beach at Santa Barbara, inhaling the spicy breeze from the Sandwich Islands, along the curved shore where the blue of the sea and the purple of the mountains remind you of the Sorrentine promontory, and then dashed away into the cañon of Montecito, among the vineyards and orange orchards and live-oaks and palms, in vales and hills all ablaze with roses and flowers of the garden and the hot - house, which bloom the year round in the gracious sea-air, would you not, we wonder, come to yourselves in the sense of a new life where it is good form to be enthusiastic and not disgraceful to be surprised? It is a far cry from Newport to Santa Barbara, and a whole world of new sensations lies on the way, experiences for which you will have no formula of experience. To take the journey is perhaps too heroic treatment for the disease of conformity—the sort of malaria of our exclusive civilization.

The Drawer is not urging this journey,

nor any break - up of the social order, for
it knows how painful a return to individuality may be. It is easier to go on in
the subordination of one's personality to
the strictly conventional life. It expects
rather to record a continually perfected
machinery, a life in which not only speech
but ideas are brought into rule. We have
had something to say occasionally of the
art of conversation, which is in danger
of being lost in the confused babel of the
reception and the chatter of the dinner-
party—the art of listening and the art of
talking both being lost. Society is taking alarm at this, and the women as usual
are leaders in a reform. Already, by reason of clubs—literary, scientific, economic
—woman is the well-informed part of our
society. In the " Conversation Lunch "
this information is now brought into use.
The lunch, and perhaps the dinner, will
no longer be the occasion of satisfying
the appetite or of gossip, but of improving talk. The giver of the lunch will fur-
nish the topic of conversation. Two persons may not speak at once ; two persons
may not talk with each other; all talk is

to be general and on the topic assigned, and while one is speaking, the others must listen. Perhaps each lady on taking her seat may find in her napkin a written slip of paper which shall be the guide to her remarks. Thus no time is to be wasted on frivolous topics. The ordinary natural flow of rejoinder and repartee, the swirling of talk around one obstacle and another, its winding and rippling here and there as individual whim suggests, will not be allowed, but all will be improving, and tend to that general culture of which we have been speaking. The ladies' lunch is not to be exactly a debating society, but an open occasion for the delivery of matured thought and the acquisition of information. The object is not to talk each other down, but to improve the mind, which, unguided, is apt to get frivolous at the convivial board. It is notorious that men by themselves at lunch or dinner usually shun grave topics and indulge in persiflage, and even descend to talk about wine and the made dishes. The women's lunch of this summer takes higher ground. It will give

Mr. Browning his final estimate; it will settle Mr. Ibsen; it will determine the suffrage question; it will adjudicate between the total abstainers and the half-way covenant of high license; it will not hesitate to cut down the tariff.

The Drawer anticipates a period of repose in all our feverish social life. We shall live more by rule and less by impulse. When we meet we shall talk on set topics, determined beforehand. By this concentration we shall be able as one man or one woman to reach the human limit of cultivation, and get rid of all the aberrations of individual assertion and feeling. By studying together in clubs, by conversing in monotone and by rule, by thinking the same things and exchanging ideas until we have none left, we shall come into that social placidity which is one dream of the nationalists—one long step towards what may be called a prairie mental condition—the slope of Kansas, where those who are five thousand feet above the sea-level seem to be no higher than those who dwell in the Missouri Valley.

THE DIRECTOIRE GOWN.

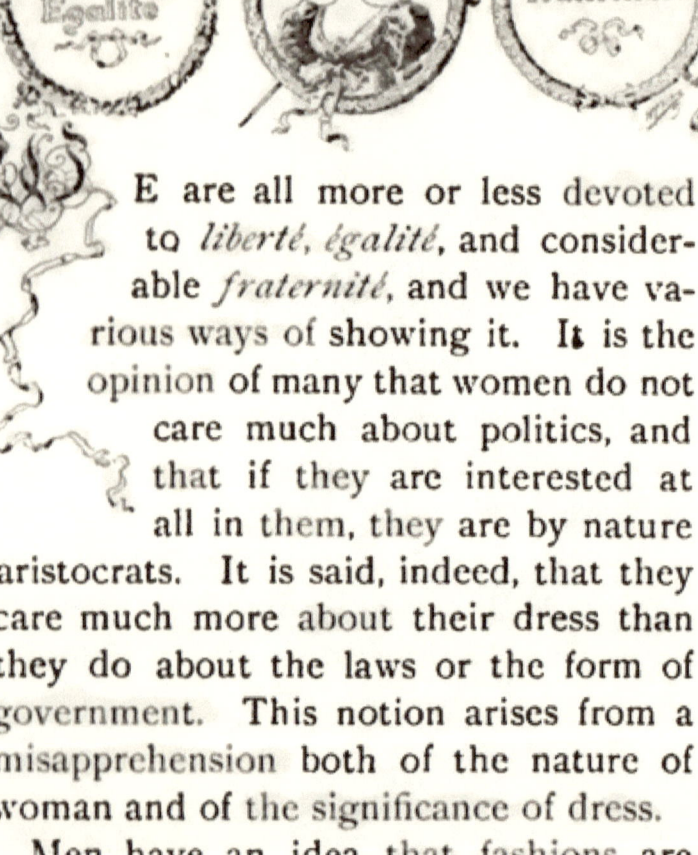

E are all more or less devoted to *liberté, égalité*, and considerable *fraternité*, and we have various ways of showing it. It is the opinion of many that women do not care much about politics, and that if they are interested at all in them, they are by nature aristocrats. It is said, indeed, that they care much more about their dress than they do about the laws or the form of government. This notion arises from a misapprehension both of the nature of woman and of the significance of dress.

Men have an idea that fashions are hap-hazard, and are dictated and guided by no fixed principles of action, and represent no great currents in politics or movements of the human mind. Women, who are exceedingly subtle in all their operations, feel that it is otherwise. They have a prescience of changes in the drift of public affairs, and a delicate sensitiveness that causes them to adjust their raiment to express these changes. Men have written a great deal in their bungling way about the philosophy of clothes. Women exhibit it, and if we should study them more and try to understand them instead of ridiculing their fashions as whims bred of an inconstant mind and mere desire for change, we would have a better apprehension of the great currents of modern political life and society.

Many observers are puzzled by the gradual and insidious return recently to the mode of the Directoire, and can see in it no significance other than weariness of some other mode. We need to recall the fact of the influence of the centenary period upon the human mind. It is nearly a century since the fashion of the Directoire. What more natural, considering the evidence that we move in spirals, if not in circles, that the signs of the anniversary of one of the most marked periods in history should be shown in feminine apparel? It is woman's way of hinting what is in the air, the spirit that is abroad in the world. It will be remembered that women took a prominent part in the destruction of the Bastile, helping, indeed, to tear down that odious structure with their own hands, the fall of which, it is well known, brought in the classic Greek and republican simplicity, the subtle meaning of the change being expressed in French gowns. Naturally there was a reaction from all this towards aristocratic privileges and exclusiveness, which went on for many years, until in France monarchy and empire followed the significant leadership of the French *modistes*. So strong was this that it passed to other countries, and in England the impulse outlasted even the Reform Bill, and skirts grew more and more bulbous, until it did not need more than three or four women to make a good-sized assembly. This was not the result of a whim about clothes, but a subtle recognition of a spirit of exclusiveness and defence abroad in the world. Each woman

became her own Bastile. Men surround-
ed it and thundered against it without
the least effect. It seemed as permanent
as the Pyramids. At every male attack
it expanded, and became more aggressive
and took up more room. Women have
such an exquisite sense of things — just
as they have now in regard to big ob-
structive hats in the theatres. They know
that most of the plays are inferior and
some of them are immoral, and they at-
tend the theatres with head-dresses that
will prevent as many people as possible
from seeing the stage and being corrupt-
ed by anything that takes place on it.
They object to the men seeing some of
the women who are now on the stage.
It happened, as to the private Bastiles,
that the women at last recognized a
change in the sociological and political
atmosphere of the world, and without
consulting any men of affairs or caring
for their opinion, down went the Bastiles.
When women attacked them, in obedience to their political instincts, they col-
lapsed like punctured balloons. Natural
woman was measurably (that is, a capac-

ity of being measured) restored to the world. And we all remember the great political revolutionary movements of 1848.

Now France is still **the** arbiter of the modes. Say what we may about Berlin, copy their fashion plates as we will, or about London, or New York, or Tokio, it is indisputable that the woman in any company who has on a Paris gown—the expression is odious, but there is no other that in these days would be comprehended—"takes the cake." It is not that **the** women care for this as a mere matter of apparel. But they are sensitive to the political atmosphere, to the philosophical significance that it has to great impending changes. We are approaching the centenary of the fall of the Bastile. **The** French have no Bastile to lay low, nor, indeed, any Tuileries to burn up; but perhaps they might get a good way ahead by demolishing Notre Dame and reducing most of Paris to ashes. Apparently they are on the eve of doing something. The women of the world may not know what it is, but they feel the approaching recurrence of a period. Their movements **are**

4

not yet decisive. It is as yet only tentatively that they adopt the mode of the Directoire. It is yet uncertain—a sort of Boulangerism in dress. But if we watch it carefully we shall be able to predict with some assurance the drift in Paris. The Directoire dress points to another period of republican simplicity, anarchy, and the rule of a popular despot.

It is a great pity, in view of this valuable instinct in women and the prophetic significance of dress, that women in the United States do not exercise their gifts with regard to their own country. We should then know at any given time whether we are drifting into Blaineism, or Clevelandism, or centralization, or free-trade, or extreme protection, or rule by corporations. We boast greatly of our smartness. It is time we were up and dressed to prove it.

THE MYSTERY OF THE SEX.

HERE appears to be a great quantity of conceit around, especially concerning women. The statement was recently set afloat that a well-known lady had admitted that George Meredith understands women better than any writer who has preceded him. This may be true, and it may be a wily statement to again throw men off the track; at any rate it contains the old assumption of a mystery, practically insoluble, about the gentler sex. Women generally encourage this notion, and men by their gingerly treatment of it seemed to accept it. But is it well founded, is there any more mystery about women than about men? Is the feminine nature any more difficult to understand that the masculine nature? Have women, conscious of inferior strength, woven this notion of mystery about themselves as a defence, or have men simply idealized them for fictitious purposes? To recur to the case cited, is there any evidence that Mr. Meredith understands human nature as exhibited in women any better than human nature in men, or is more consistent in the production of one than of the other?

Historically it would be interesting to trace the rise of this notion of woman as an enigma. The savage races do not appear to have it. A woman to the North American Indian is a simple affair, dealt with without circumlocution. In the Bible records there is not much mystery about her; there are many tributes to her noble qualities, and some pretty severe and uncomplimentary things are said about her, but there is little affectation of not understanding her. She may be a prophetess, or a consoler, or a snare, but she is no more " deceitful and desperately wicked " than anybody else. There is nothing mysterious about her first recorded performance. Eve trusted the serpent, and Adam trusted Eve. The mystery was in the serpent. There is no evidence that the ancient Egyptian woman was more difficult to comprehend than the Egyptian man. They were both doubtless wily as highly civilized people are apt to be; the "serpent of old Nile" was in them both. Is it in fact till we come to mediæval times, and the chivalric age, that women are set up as being more incomprehensible than men? That is, less logical, more whimsical, more uncertain in their mental processes? The playwriters and essayists of the seventeenth and eighteenth centuries "worked" this notion continually. They always took an investigating and speculating attitude towards women, that fostered the conceit of their separateness and veiled personality. Every woman was supposed to be playing a part behind a mask. Montaigne is always investigating woman as a mystery. It is, for instance, a mystery he does not relish that, as he says, women commonly reserve the publication of their vehement affections for their husbands till they have lost them; then the woful countenance "looks not so much back as forward, and is intended rather to get a new husband than to lament the old." And he tells this story: "When I was a boy, a very beautiful and virtuous lady who is yet living, and the widow of a prince, had, I know not what, more ornament in her dress than our laws of widowhood will well allow, which being reproached with as a great indecency, she made answer 'that it was because she was not cultivating more friendships, and would never marry again.'" This cynical view of woman, as well as the extravagantly complimentary one sometimes taken by the poets, was based upon the notion that woman was an unexplainable being. When she herself adopted the idea is uncertain.

Of course all this has a very practical bearing upon modern life, the position of women in it, and the so-called reforms. If woman is so different from man to the extent of being an unexplainable mystery, science ought to determine the exact state of the case, and ascertain if there is any remedy for it. If it is only a literary creation, we ought to know it. Science could tell, for instance, whether there is a peculiarity in the nervous system, any complications in the nervous centres, by which the telegraphic action of the will gets crossed, so that, for example, in reply to a proposal of marriage, the intended "Yes" gets delivered as "No." Is it true that the mental process in one sex is intuitive, and in the other logical, with every link necessary and visible? Is it true, as the romancers teach, that the mind in one sex acts indirectly and in the other directly, or is this indirect process only characteristic of exceptions in both sexes? Investigation ought to find this out, so that we can adjust the fit occupations for both sexes on a scientific basis. We are floundering about now in a sea of doubt. As society becomes more complicated, women will become a greater and greater mystery, or rather will be regarded so by themselves and be treated so by men.

Who can tell how much this notion of mystery in the sex stands in the way of its free advancement all along the line?

Suppose the proposal were made to women to exchange being mysterious for the ballot? Would they do it? Or have they a sense of power in the possession of this conceded incomprehensibility that they would not lay down for any visible insignia of that power? And if the novelists and essayists have raised a mist about the sex, which it willingly masquerades in, is it not time that the scientists should determine whether the mystery exists in nature or only in the imagination?

THE CLOTHES OF FICTION.

HE Drawer has never underval-
ued clothes. Whatever other
heresies it may have had, however it may have insisted that
the more a woman learns, the
more she knows of books, the higher her
education is carried in all the knowledges,
the more interesting she will be, not only for
an hour, but as a companion for life, it has
never said that she is less attractive when
dressed with taste and according to the
season. Love itself could scarcely be expected to survive a winter hat worn after
Easter. And the philosophy of this is not
on the surface, nor applicable to women
only. In this the highest of created things
are under a law having a much wider ap-

plication. Take as an item novels, the works of fiction, which have become an absolute necessity in the modern world, as necessary to divert the mind loaded with care and under actual strain as to fill the vacancy in otherwise idle brains. They have commonly a summer and a winter apparel. The publishers understand this. As certainly as the birds appear, comes the crop of summer novels, fluttering down upon the stalls, in procession through the railway trains, littering the drawing-room tables, in light paper covers, ornamental, attractive in colors and fanciful designs, as welcome and grateful as the girls in muslin. When the thermometer is in the eighties, anything heavy and formidable is distasteful. The house-keeper knows we want few solid dishes, but salads and cooling drinks. The publisher knows that we want our literature (or what passes for that) in light array. In the winter we prefer the boards and the rich heavy binding, however light the tale may be; but in the summer, though the fiction be as grave and tragic as wandering love and bankruptcy, we would have it come to us lightly clad — out of stays, as it were.

It would hardly be worth while to refer to this taste in the apparel of our fiction did it not have deep and esoteric suggestions, and could not the novelists themselves get a hint from it. Is it realized how much depends upon the clothes that are worn by the characters in the novels — clothes put on not only to exhibit the inner life of the characters, but to please the readers who are to associate with them? It is true that there are novels that almost do away with the necessity of fashion magazines and fashion plates in the family, so faithful are they in the latest millinery details, and so fully do they satisfy the longing of all of us to know what is *chic* for the moment. It is pretty well understood, also, that women, and even men, are made to exhibit the deepest passions and the tenderest emotions in the crises of their lives by the clothes they put on. How the woman in such a crisis hesitates before her wardrobe, and at last chooses just what will express her innermost feeling! Does she dress for her lover as she dresses to receive her lawyer who has come to inform her that she is living beyond her income? Would not the lover be spared time and pain if he knew, as the novelist knows, whether the young lady is dressing for a rejection or an acceptance? Why does the lady intending suicide always throw on a water-proof when she steals out of the house to drown herself? The novelist knows the deep significance of every article of toilet, and nature teaches him to array his characters for the summer novel in the airy draperies suitable to the season. It is only good art that the cover of the novel and the covers of the characters shall be in harmony. He knows, also, that the characters in the winter novel must be adequately protected. We speak, of course, of the season stories. Novels that are to run through a year, or maybe many years, and are to set forth the passions and trials of changing age and varying circumstance, require different treatment and wider millinery knowledge. They are naturally more expensive. The wardrobe required in an all-round novel would bankrupt most of us.

But to confine ourselves to the season novel, it is strange that some one has not invented the patent adjustable story that with a slight change would do for summer or winter, following the broad hint of the publishers, who hasten in May to throw whatever fiction they have on hand into summer clothes. The winter novel, by this invention, could be easily fitted for summer wear. All the novelist need do would be to change the clothes of his characters. And in the autumn, if the novel proved popular, he could change again, with the advantage of being in the latest fashion. It would only be necessary to alter a few sentences in a few of the stereotype pages. Of course this would make necessary other slight alterations, for no kind-hearted writer would be cruel to his own creations, and expose them to the vicissitudes of the seasons. He could insert " rain " for " snow," and " green leaves " for " skeleton branches," make a few verbal changes of that sort, and regulate the thermometer. It would

5

cost very little to adjust the novel in this way to any season. It is worth thinking of.

And this leads to a remark upon the shocking indifference of some novelists to the ordinary comfort of their characters. In practical life we cannot, but in his realm the novelist can, control the weather. He can make it generally pleasant. We do not object to a terrific thunder-shower now and then, as the sign of despair and a lost soul, but perpetual drizzle and grayness and inclemency are tedious to the reader, who has enough bad weather in his private experience. The English are greater sinners in this respect than we are. They seem to take a brutal delight in making it as unpleasant as possible for their fictitious people. There is *R—b—rt 'lsm—r'*, for example. External trouble is piled on to the internal. The characters are in a perpetual soak. There is not a dry rag on any of them, from the beginning of the book to the end. They are sent out in all weathers, and are drenched every day. Often their wet clothes are frozen on them;

they are exposed to cutting winds and sleet in their faces, bedrabbled in damp grass, stood against slippery fences, with hail and frost lowering their vitality, and expected under these circumstances to make love and be good Christians. Drenched and wind-blown for years, that is what they are. It may be that this treatment has excited the sympathy of the world, but is it legitimate? Has a novelist the right to subject his creations to tortures that he would not dare to inflict upon his friends? It is no excuse to say that this is normal English weather; it is not the office of fiction to intensify and rub in the unavoidable evils of life. The modern spirit of consideration for fictitious characters that prevails with regard to dress ought to extend in a reasonable degree to their weather. This is not a strained corollary to the demand for an appropriately costumed novel.

THE BROAD A.

I T cannot for a moment be supposed that the Drawer would discourage self-culture and refinement of manner and of speech. But it would not hesitate to give a note of warning if it believed that the present devotion to literature and the pursuits of the mind were likely, by the highest authorities, to be considered bad form. In an intellectually inclined city (not in the north-east) a club of ladies has been formed for the cultivation of the broad *a* in speech. Sporadic efforts have hitherto been made for the proper treatment of this letter of the alphabet with individual success, especially with those who have been in England, or have known English men and women of the broadgauge variety. Discerning travellers have made the American pronunciation of the letter *a* a reproach to the republic, that is to say, a means of distinguishing a native of this country. The true American aspires to be cosmopolitan, and does not want to be "spotted"—if that word may be used—in society by any peculiarity of speech, that is, by any American peculiarity. Why, at the bottom of the matter, a narrow *a* should be a disgrace it is not easy to see, but it needs no reason if fashion or authority condemns it. This country is so spread out, without any social or literary centre universally recognized as such, and the narrow *a* has become so prevalent, that even fashion finds it difficult to reform it. The best people, who are determined to broaden all their *a*'s, will forget in moments of excitement, and fall back into old habits. It requires constant vigilance to keep the letter *a* flattened out. It is in vain that scholars have pointed out that in the use of this letter lies the main difference between the English and the American speech ; either Americans generally do not care if this is the fact, or fashion can only work a reform in a limited number of people. It seems, therefore, necessary that there should be an organized effort to deal with this pronunciation, and clubs will no doubt be formed all over the country, in imitation of the one mentioned, until the broad *a* will become as common as flies in summer. When this result is attained it will be time to attack the sound of *u* with clubs, and make universal the French sound. In time the American pronunciation will become as superior to all others as are the American sewing-machines and reapers. In the Broad A Club every member who misbehaves—that is, mispronounces—is fined a nickel for each offence. Of course in the beginning there is a good deal of revenue from this source, but the revenue diminishes as the club improves, so that we have the anomaly of its failure to be self-supporting in proportion to its excellence. Just now if these clubs could suddenly become universal, and the penalty be enforced, we could have the means of paying off the national debt in a year.

We do not wish to attach too much

importance to this movement, but rather to suggest to a continent yearning for culture in letters and in speech whether it may not be carried too far. The reader will remember that there came a time in Athens when culture could mock at itself, and the rest of the country may be warned in time of a possible departure from good form in devotion to language and literature by the present attitude of modern Athens. Probably there is no esoteric depth in literature or religion, no refinement in intellectual luxury, that this favored city has not sounded. It is certainly significant, therefore, when the priestesses and devotees of mental superiority there turn upon it and rend it, when they are heartily tired of the whole literary business. There is always this danger when anything is passionately pursued as a fashion, that it will one day cease to be the fashion. Plato and Buddha and even Emerson become in time like a last season's fashion plate. Even a "friend of the spirit" will have to go. Culture is certain to mock itself in time.

The clubs for the improvement of the

mind—the female mind—and of speech, which no doubt had their origin in modern Athens, should know, then, that it is the highest mark of female culture now in that beautiful town to despise culture, to affect the gayest and most joyous ignorance—ignorance of books, of all forms of so-called intellectual development, and all literary men, women, and productions whatsoever ! This genuine movement of freedom may be a real emancipation. If it should reach the metropolis, what a relief it might bring to thousands who are, under a high sense of duty, struggling to advance the intellectual life. There is this to be said, however, that it is only the very brightest people, those who have no need of culture, who have in fact passed beyond all culture, who can take this position in regard to it, and actually revel in the delights of ignorance. One must pass into a calm place when he is beyond the desire to know anything or to do anything.

It is a chilling thought, unless one can rise to the highest philosophy of life, that even the broad *a*, when it is attained, may not be a permanence. Let it be common, and what distinction will there be in it? When devotion to study, to the reading of books, to conversation on improving topics, becomes a universal fashion, is it not evident that one can only keep a leadership in fashion by throwing the whole thing overboard, and going forward into the natural gayety of life, which cares for none of these things? We suppose the Constitution of the United States will stand if the day comes —nay, now is—when the women of Chicago call the women of Boston frivolous, and the women of Boston know their immense superiority and advancement in being so, but it would be a blank surprise to the country generally to know that it was on the wrong track. The fact is that culture in this country is full of surprises, and so doubles and feints and comes back upon itself that the most diligent recorder can scarcely note its changes. The Drawer can only warn ; it cannot advise.

CHEWING GUM.

IN language that is unfortunately understood by the greater portion of the people who speak English, thousands are saying on the first of January—in 1890, a far-off date that it is wonderful any one has lived to see —" Let us have a new deal!" It is a natural exclamation, and does not necessarily mean any change of purpose. It always seems to a man that if he could shuffle the cards he could increase his advantages in the game of life, and, to continue the figure which needs so little explanation, it usually appears to him that he could play anybody else's hand better than his own. In all the good resolutions of the new year, then, it happens that perhaps the most sincere is the determination to get a better hand. Many mistake this for repentance and an intention to reform, when generally it is only the desire for a new shuffle of the cards. Let us have a fresh pack and a new deal, and start fair. It seems idle, therefore, for the moralist to indulge in a homily about annual good intentions, and habits that ought to be dropped or acquired, on the first of January. He can do little more than comment on the passing show.

It will be admitted that if the world at this date is not socially reformed it is not the fault of the Drawer, and for the reason that it has been not so much a critic as an explainer and encourager. It is in the latter character that it undertakes to defend and justify a national industry that has become very important within the past ten years. A great deal of capital is invested in it, and millions of people are actively employed in it. The varieties of chewing gum that are manufactured would be a matter of surprise to those who have paid no attention to the subject, and who may suppose that the millions of mouths they see engaged in its mastication have a common and vulgar taste. From the fact that it can be obtained at the apothecary's, an impression has got abroad that it is medicinal. This is not true. The medical profession do not use it, and what distinguishes it from drugs—that they also do not use—is the fact that they do not prescribe it. It is neither a narcotic nor a stimulant. It cannot strictly be said to soothe or to excite. The habit of using it differs totally from that of the chewing of tobacco or the dipping of snuff. It might, by a purely mechanical operation, keep a person awake, but no one could go to sleep chewing gum. It is in itself neither tonic nor sedative. It is to be noticed also that the gum habit differs from the tobacco habit in that the aromatic and elastic substance is masticated, while the tobacco never is, and that the mastication leads to nothing except more mastication. The task is one that can never be finished. The amount of energy expended in this process if capitalized or conserved would produce great results.

6

Of course the individual does little, but if the power evolved by the practice in a district school could be utilized, it would suffice to run the kindergarten department. The writer has seen a railway car —say in the West—filled with young women, nearly every one of whose jaws and pretty mouths was engaged in this pleasing occupation; and so much power was generated that it would, if applied, have kept the car in motion if the steam had been shut off—at least it would have furnished the motive for illuminating the car by electricity.

This national industry is the subject of constant detraction, satire, and ridicule by the newspaper press. This is because it is not understood, and it may be because it is mainly a female accomplishment: the few men who chew gum may be supposed to do so by reason of gallantry. There might be no more sympathy with it in the press if the real reason for the practice were understood, but it would be treated more respectfully. Some have said that the practice arises from nervousness—the idle desire to be

busy without doing anything—and because it fills up the pauses of vacuity in
conversation. But this would not fully
account for the practice of it in solitude.
Some have regarded it as in obedience to
the feminine instinct for the cultivation
of patience and self-denial—patience in a
fruitless activity, and self-denial in the
eternal act of mastication without swal-
lowing. It is no more related to these
virtues than it is to the habit of the re-
flective cow in chewing her cud. The
cow would never chew gum. The explanation is a more philosophical one,
and relates to a great modern social
movement. It is to strengthen and develop and make more masculine the lower jaw. The critic who says that this is
needless, that the inclination in women
to talk would adequately develop this,
misses the point altogether. Even if it
could be proved that women are greater
chatterers than men, the critic would
gain nothing. Women have talked freely
since creation, but it remains true that a
heavy, strong lower jaw is a distinctively
masculine characteristic. It is remarked

that if a woman has a strong lower jaw she is like a man. Conversation does not create this difference, nor remove it; for the development of a lower jaw in women constant mechanical exercise of the muscles is needed. Now, a spirit of emancipation, of emulation, is abroad, as it ought to be, for the regeneration of the world. It is sometimes called the coming to the front of woman in every act and occupation that used to belong almost exclusively to man. It is not necessary to say a word to justify this. But it is often accompanied by a misconception, namely, that it is necessary for woman to be like man, not only in habits, but in certain physical characteristics. No woman desires a beard, because a beard means care and trouble, and would detract from feminine beauty, but to have a strong and, in appearance, a resolute underjaw may be considered a desirable note of masculinity, and of masculine power and privilege, in the good time coming. Hence the cultivation of it by the chewing of gum is a recognizable and reasonable instinct, and the practice can be defended as neither a whim nor a vain waste of energy and nervous force. In a generation or two it may be laid aside as no longer necessary, or men may be compelled to resort to it to preserve their supremacy.

WOMEN IN CONGRESS.

T does not seem to be decided yet whether women are to take the Senate or the House at Washington in the new development of what is called the dual government. There are disadvantages in both. The members of the Senate are so few that the women of the country would not be adequately represented in it; and the Chamber in which the House meets is too large for women to make speeches in with any pleasure to themselves or their hearers. This last objection is, however, frivolous, for the speeches will be printed in the *Record;* and it is as easy to count women on a vote as men. There is nothing in the objection, either, that the Chamber would need to be remodelled, and the smoking-rooms be turned into Day Nurseries. The coming woman will not smoke, to be sure; neither will she, in coming forward to take charge of the government, plead the Baby Act. Only those women, we are told, would be elected to Congress whose age and position enable them to devote themselves exclusively to politics. The question, therefore, of taking to themselves the Senate or the House will be decided by the women themselves upon other grounds—as to whether they wish to take the initiative in legislation and hold the power of the purse, or whether they prefer to act as a check, to exercise the high treaty-making power, and to have a voice in selecting the women who shall be sent to represent us abroad. Other things being equal, women will naturally select the Upper House, and especially as that will give them an opportunity to reject any but the the most competent women for the Supreme Bench. The irreverent scoffers at our Supreme Court have in the past complained (though none do now) that there were "old women" in gowns on the bench. There would be no complaint of the kind in the future. The judges would be as pretty as those who assisted in the judgment of Paris, with changed functions; there would be no monotony in the dress, and the Supreme Bench would be one of the most attractive spectacles in Washington. When the judges as well as the advocates are Portias, the law will be an agreeable occupation.

This is, however, mere speculation. We do not understand that it is the immediate purpose of women to take the whole government, though some extravagant expectations are raised by the admission of new States that are ruled by women. They may wish to divide—and conquer. One plan is, instead of dual Chambers of opposite sexes, to mingle in both the Senate and the House. And this is more likely to be the plan adopted, because the revolution is not to be violent, and, indeed,

cannot take place without some readjust-
ment of the home life. We have at present what Charles Reade would have called
only a right-handed civilization. To speak
metaphorically, men cannot use their left
hands, or, to drop the metaphor, before
the government can be fully reorganized
men must learn to do women's work. It
may be a fair inference from this movement that women intend to abandon the
sacred principle of Home Rule. This
abandonment is foreshadowed in a recent
election in a small Western city, where
the female voters made a clean sweep,
elected an entire city council of women
and most of the other officers, including
the police judge and the mayor. The
latter lady, by one of those intrusions of
nature which reform is not yet able to
control, became a mother and a mayor
the same week. Her husband had been
city clerk, and held over; but fortunately
an arrangement was made with him to
stay at home and take care of the baby,
unofficially, while the mayor attends to
her public duties. Thus the city clerk
will gradually be initiated into the duties

of home rule, and when the mayor is elected to Congress, he will be ready to accompany her to Washington and keep house. The imagination likes to dwell upon this, for the new order is capable of infinite extension. When the State takes care of all the children in government nurseries, and the mayor has taken her place in the United States Senate, her husband, if he has become sufficiently reformed and feminized, may go to the House, and the reunited family of two, clubbing their salaries, can live in great comfort.

All this can be easily arranged, whether we are to have a dual government of sexes or a mixed House and Senate. The real difficulty is about a single Executive. Neither sex will be willing to yield to the other this vast power. We might elect a man and wife President and Vice-President, but the Vice-President, of whatever sex, could not well preside over the Senate and in the White House at the same time. It is true that the Constitution provides that the President and Vice-President shall not be of the same State, but residence can be acquired to get over this as easily as to obtain a divorce; and a Constitution that insists upon speaking of the President as "he" is too antiquated to be respected. When the President is a woman, it can matter little whether her husband or some other woman presides in the Senate. Even the reformers will hardly insist upon two Presidents in order to carry out the equality idea, so that we are probably anticipating difficulties that will not occur in practice.

The Drawer has only one more practical suggestion. As the right of voting carries with it the right to hold any elective office, a great change must take place in Washington life. Now for some years the divergence of society and politics has been increasing at the capital. With women in both Houses, and on the Supreme Bench, and at the heads of the departments, social and political life will become one and the same thing; receptions and afternoon teas will be held in the Senate and House, and political caucuses in all the drawing-rooms. And then life will begin to be interesting.

SHALL WOMEN PROPOSE?

HE shyness of man—meaning the "other sex" referred to in the woman's journals—has often been noticed in novels, and sometimes in real life. This shyness is, however, so exceptional as to be suspicious. The shy young man may provoke curiosity, but he does not always inspire respect. Roughly estimated, shyness is not considered a manly quality, while it is one of the most pleasing and attractive of the feminine traits, and there is something pathetic in the expression "He is as shy as a girl;" it may appeal for sympathy and the exercise of the protective instinct in women. Unfortunately it is a little discredited, so many of the old plays turning upon its assumption by young blades who are no better than they should be.

7

What would be the effect upon the masculine character and comfort if this shyness should become general, as it may in
a contingency that is already on the hori-
zon? We refer, of course, to the suggestion, coming from various quarters, that
women should propose. The reasonable-
ness of this suggestion may not lie on the
surface; it may not be deduced from the
uniform practice, beginning with the prim-
itive men and women; it may not be in-
ferred from the open nature of the two
sexes (for the sake of argument two
sexes must still be insisted on); but it is
found in the advanced civilization with
which we are struggling. Why should
not women propose? Why should they
be at a disadvantage in an affair which
concerns the happiness of the whole life?
They have as much right to a choice as
men, and to an opportunity to exercise
it. Why should they occupy a negative
position, and be restricted, in making the
most important part of their career, wholly to the choice implied in refusals? In
fact, marriage really concerns them more
than it does men; they have to bear the

chief of its burdens. A wide and free choice for them would, then, seem to be only fair. Undeniably a great many men are inattentive, unobserving, immersed in some absorbing pursuit, undecided, and at times bashful, and liable to fall into union with women who happen to be near them, rather than with those who are conscious that they would make them the better wives. Men, unaided by the finer feminine instincts of choice, are so apt to be deceived. In fact, man's inability to " match " anything is notorious. If he cannot be trusted in the matter of worsted-work, why should he have such distinctive liberty in the most important matter of his life? Besides, there are many men—and some of the best—who get into a habit of not marrying at all, simply because the right woman has not presented herself at the right time. Perhaps, if women had the open privilege of selection, many a good fellow would be rescued from miserable isolation, and perhaps also many a noble woman whom chance, or a stationary position, or the inertia of the other sex, has left to bloom alone, and waste her sweetness on relations, would be the centre of a charming home, furnishing the finest spectacle seen in this uphill world—a woman exercising gracious hospitality, and radiating to a circle far beyond her home the influence of her civilizing personality. For, notwithstanding all the centrifugal forces of this age, it is probable that the home will continue to be the fulcrum on which women will move the world.

It may be objected that it would be unfair to add this opportunity to the already overpowering attractions of woman, and that man would be put at an immense disadvantage, since he might have too much gallantry, or not enough presence of mind, to refuse a proposal squarely and fascinatingly made, although his judgment scarcely consented, and his ability to support a wife were more than doubtful. Women would need to exercise a great deal of prudence and discretion, or there would be something like a panic, and a cry along the male line of *Sauve qui peut;* for it is matter of record that the bravest men will sometimes run away from danger on a sudden impulse.

This prospective social revolution suggests many inquiries. What would be the effect upon the female character and disposition of a possible, though not probable, refusal, or of several refusals? Would she become embittered and desperate, and act as foolishly as men often do? Would her own sex be considerate, and give her a fair field if they saw she was paying attention to a young man, or an old one? And what effect would this change in relations have upon men? Would it not render that sporadic shyness of which we have spoken epidemic? Would it frighten men, rendering their position less stable in their own eyes, or would it feminize them — that is, make them retiring, blushing, self-conscious beings? And would this change be of any injury to them in their necessary fight for existence in this pushing world? What would be the effect upon courtship if both the men and the women approached each other as wooers? In ordinary transactions one is a buyer and one is a seller—to put it coarsely. If seller met seller and buyer met buyer, trade

would languish. But this figure cannot
be continued, for there is no romance in
a bargain of any sort; and what we should
most fear in a scientific age is the loss of
romance.

This is, however, mere speculation.
The serious aspect of the proposed
change is the effect it will have upon the
character of men, who are not enough
considered in any of these discussions.
The revolution will be a radical one in
one respect. We may admit that in the
future woman can take care of herself,
but how will it be with man, who has had
little disciplinary experience of adversity,
simply because he has been permitted to
have his own way. Heretofore his life
has had a stimulus. When he proposes to
a woman, he in fact says: " I am able to
support you; I am able to protect you
from the rough usage of the world; I am
strong and ambitious, and eager to take
upon myself the lovely bondage of this
responsibility. I offer you this love because I feel the courage and responsibility of my position." That is the manly
part of it. What effect will it have upon

his character to be waiting round, unselected and undecided, until some woman comes to him, and fixes her fascinating eyes upon him, and says, in effect: "I can support you; I can defend you. Have no fear of the future; I will be at once your shield and your backbone. I take the responsibility of my choice." There are a great many men now, who have sneaked into their positions by a show of courage, who are supported one way and another by women. It might be humiliating to know just how many men live by the labors of their wives. And what would be the effect upon the character of man if the choice, and the responsibility of it, and the support implied by it in marriage, were generally transferred to woman?

FROCKS AND THE STAGE.

THE condescension to literature and to the stage is one of the notable characteristics of this agreeable time. We have to admit that literature is rather the fashion, without the violent presumption that the author and the writer have the same social position that is conferred by money, or by the mysterious virtue there is in pedigree. A person does not lose caste by using the pen, or even by taking the not-needed pay for using it. To publish a book or to have an article accepted by a magazine may give a sort of social distinction, either as an exhibition of a certain unexpected capacity or a social eccentricity. It is hardly too much to say that it has become the fashion to write, as it used to be to dance the minuet well,

or to use the broadsword, or to stand a
gentlemanly mill with a renowned bruiser.
Of course one ought not to do this pro-
fessionally exactly, ought not to prepare
for doing it by study and severe discipline,
by training for it as for a trade, but simply to toss it off easily, as one makes a
call, or pays a compliment, or drives four-
in-hand. One does not need to have that
interior impulse which drives a poor devil
of an author to express himself, that
something to say which torments the poet
into extreme irritability unless he can be
rid of it, that noble hunger for fame which
comes from a consciousness of the possession of vital thought and emotion. The
beauty of this condescension to literature
of which we speak is that it has that quality of spontaneity that does not presup-
pose either a capacity or a call. There is
no mystery about the craft. One resolves
to write a book, as he might to take a
journey or to practise on the piano, and
the thing is done. Everybody can write,
at least everybody does write. It is a
wonderful time for literature. The Queen
of England writes for it, the Queen of

Roumania writes for it, the Shah of Persia writes for it, Lady Brassey, the yachtswoman, wrote for it, Congressmen write for it, peers write for it. The novel is the common recreation of ladies of rank, and where is the young woman in this country who has not tried her hand at a romance or made a cast at a popular magazine? The effect of all this upon literature is expansive and joyous. Superstition about any mystery in the art has nearly disappeared. It is a common observation that if persons fail in everything else, if they are fit for nothing else, they can at least write. It is such an easy occupation, and the remuneration is in such disproportion to the expenditure! Isn't it indeed the golden era of letters? If only the letters were gold!

If there is any such thing remaining as a guild of authors, somewhere on the back seats, witnessing this marvellous Kingdom Come of Literature, there must also be a little bunch of actors, born for the stage, who see with mixed feelings their arena taken possession of by fairer if not more competent players. These players are not to be confounded with the play-actors whom the Puritans denounced, nor with those trained to the profession in the French capital. In the United States and in England we are born to enter upon any avocation, thank Heaven! without training for it. We have not in this country any such obstacle to universal success as the Théâtre Français, but Providence has given us, for wise purposes no doubt, Private Theatricals (not always so private as they should be), which domesticate the drama, and supply the stage with some of the most beautiful and best dressed performers the world has ever seen. Whatever they may say of it, it is a gallant and a susceptible age, and all men bow to loveliness, and all women recognize a talent for clothes. We do not say that there is not such a thing as dramatic art, and that there are not persons who need as severe training before they attempt to personate nature in art as the painter must undergo who attempts to transfer its features to his canvas. But the taste of the age must be taken into account. The public does not demand that an actor shall come in at a private door and climb a steep staircase to get to the stage. When a Star from the Private Theatricals descends upon the boards, with the arms of Venus and the throat of Juno, and a wardrobe got out of Paris and through our stingy Custom-house in forty trunks, the plodding actor, who has depended upon art, finds out, what he has been all the time telling us, that all the world's a stage, and men and women merely players. Art is good in its way; but what about a perfect figure? and is not dressing an art? Can training give one an elegant form, and study command the services of a man milliner? The stage is broadened out and re-enforced by a new element. What went ye out for to see? A person clad in fine raiment, to be sure. Some of the critics may growl a little, and hint at the invasion of art by fashionable life, but the editor, whose motto is that the newspaper is made for man, not man for the newspaper, understands what is required in this inspiring histrionic movement, and when a lovely woman condescends to step from the drawing-room to the stage he confines his descriptions to her person, and does not bother about her capacity; **and** instead of wearying us with a list of her plays and performances, he gives us a column about her dresses in beautiful language that shows us how closely allied poetry **is** to tailoring. Can the lady act? Why, simple - minded, she has nearly **a** hundred frocks, each one a dream, a conception of genius, a vaporous idea, one might say, which will reveal more beauty **than** it hides, and teach the spectator that art is simply nature adorned. Rachel in all her glory was not adorned like one of these. We have changed all that. The actress used to have **a** rehearsal. She now **has** an "opening."

Does it require nowadays, then, no special talent or gift to go on the stage? No more, we can assure our readers, than it does to write a book. But homely people and poor people can write books. **As yet** they cannot act.

ALTRUISM.

CHRISTMAS is supposed to be an altruistic festival. Then, if ever, we allow ourselves to go out to others in sympathy expressed by gifts and good wishes. Then self-forgetfulness in the happiness of others becomes a temporary fashion. And we find—do we not?—the indulgence of the feeling so remunerative that we wish there were other days set apart to it. We can even understand those people who get a private satisfaction in being good on other days besides Sunday. There is a common notion that this Christmas altruistic sentiment is particularly shown towards the unfortunate and the dependent by those more prosperous, and in what is called a better social position. We are exhorted on this day to remember the poor. We need to be reminded rather to remember the rich, the lonely, not-easy-to-be-satisfied rich, whom we do not always have with us. The Drawer never sees a very rich person that it does not long to give him something, some token, the value of which is not estimated by its cost, that should be a consoling evidence to him that he has not lost sympathetic touch with ordinary humanity. There is a great deal of sympathy afloat in the world, but it is especially shown downward in the social scale. We treat our servants—supposing that we are society—better than we treat each other. If we did not, they would leave us. We are kinder to the unfortunate or the dependent than to each other, and we have more charity for them.

The Drawer is not indulging in any indiscriminate railing at society. There is society and society. There is that undefined something, more like a machine than an aggregate of human sensibilities, which is set going in a "season," or at a watering-place, or permanently selects itself for certain social manifestations. It is this that needs a missionary to infuse into it sympathy and charity. If it were indeed a machine and not made up of sensitive personalities, it would not be to its members so selfish and cruel. It would be less an ambitious scramble for place and favor, less remorseless towards the unsuccessful, not so harsh and hard and supercilious. In short, it would be much more agreeable if it extended to its own members something of the consideration and sympathy that it gives to those it regards as its inferiors. It seems to think that good-breeding and good form are separable from kindliness and sympathy and helpfulness. Tender-hearted and charitable enough all the individuals of this "society" are to persons below them in fortune or position, let us allow, but how are they to each other? Nothing can be ruder or less considerate of the feelings of others than much of that which is called good society, and this is why the Drawer desires to turn the altruistic sentiment of the world upon it in this season, set apart by common consent for usefulness. Unfortunate are the fortunate if they are lifted into a sphere which is sapless of delicacy of feeling for its own. Is this an intangible matter? Take hospitality, for instance. Does it consist in astonishing the invited, in overwhelming him with a sense of your own wealth, or felicity, or family, or cleverness even; in trying to absorb him in your concerns, your successes, your possessions, in simply what interests you? However delightful all these may be, it is an offence to his individuality to insist that he shall admire at the point of the social bayonet. How do you treat the stranger? Do you adapt yourself and your surroundings to him, or insist that he shall adapt himself to you? How often does the stranger, the guest, sit in helpless agony in your circle (all of whom know each other) at table or in the drawing-room, isolated and separate, because all the talk is local and personal, about your little world, and the affairs of your clique, and your petty interests, in which he or she cannot possibly join? Ah! the Sioux Indian would not be so cruel as that to a guest, There is no more refined torture to a sensitive person than that. Is it only thoughtlessness? It is more than that. It is a want of sympathy of the heart, or it is a lack of intelligence and broad-minded interest in affairs of the world and in other people. It is this trait—absorption in self—pervading society more or less, that makes it so unsatisfactory to most people in it. Just a want of human interest; people do not come in contact.

Avid pursuit of wealth, or what is called pleasure, perhaps makes people hard to each other, and infuses into the higher social life, which should be the most unselfish and enjoyable life, a certain vulgarity, similar to that noticed in well-bred tourists scrambling for the seats on top of a mountain coach. A person of refinement and sensibility and intelligence, cast into the company of the select, the country-house, the radiant, twelve-button society, has been struck with infinite pity for it, and asks the Drawer to do something about it. The Drawer cannot do anything about it. It can only ask the prayers of all good people on Christmas Day

for the rich. As we said, we do not have
them with us always—they are here to-
day, they are gone to Canada to-morrow.
But this is, of course, current facetious-
ness. The rich are as good as anybody
else, according to their lights, and if what
is called society were as good and as kind
to itself as it is to the poor, it would be
altogether enviable. We are not of those
who say that in this case charity would
cover a multitude of sins, but a diffusion
in society of the Christmas sentiment of
good-will and kindliness to itself would
tend to make universal the joy on the return of this season.

HE Drawer would like to emphasize the noble, self-sacrificing spirit of American women. There are none like them in the world. They take up all the burdens of artificial foreign usage, where social caste prevails, and bear them with a heroism worthy of a worse cause. They indeed represent these usages to be a burden almost intolerable, and yet they submit to them with a grace and endurance all their own. Probably there is no harder-worked person than a lady in the season, let us say in Washington, where the etiquette of visiting is carried to a perfection that it does not reach even in New York, Boston, or Philadelphia, and where woman's effort to keep the social fabric together requires more expenditure of intellect

and of physical force than was needed
to protect the capital in its peril a quar-
ter of a century ago. When this cruel
war is over, the monument to the wom-
en who perished in it will need to be
higher than that to the Father of his
Country. Merely in the item of keeping
an account of the visits paid and due, a
woman needs a book-keeper. Only to
know the etiquette of how and when and
to whom and in what order the visits are
to be paid is to be well educated in a
matter that assumes the first importance
in her life. This is, however, only a de-
tail of book-keeping and of memory; to
pay and receive, or evade, these visits of
ceremony is a work which men can admire without the power to imitate; even
on the supposition that a woman has nothing else to do, it calls for our humble gratitude and a recognition of the largeness of
nature that can put aside any duties to
husband or children in devotion to the
public welfare. The futile round of society life while it lasts admits of no rival.
It seems as important as the affairs of the
government. The Drawer is far from say-

ing that it is not. Perhaps no one can tell what confusion would fall into all the political relations if the social relations of the capital were not kept oiled by the system of exchange of fictitious courtesies among the women; and it may be true that society at large—men are so apt, when left alone, to relapse — would fall into barbarism if our pasteboard conventions were neglected. All honor to the self-sacrifice of woman !

What a beautiful civilization ours is, supposed to be growing in intelligence and simplicity, and yet voluntarily taking upon itself this artificial burden in an already overtaxed life! The angels in heaven must admire and wonder. The cynic wants to know what is gained for any rational being when a city full of women undertake to make and receive formal visits with persons whom for the most part they do not wish to see. What is gained, he asks, by leaving cards with all these people and receiving their cards? When a woman makes her tedious rounds, why is she always relieved to find people not in ? When she can count upon her ten fingers the people she wants to see, why should she pretend to want to see the others? Is any one deceived by it? Does anybody regard it as anything but a sham and a burden? Much the cynic knows about it! Is it not necessary to keep up what is called society? Is it not necessary to have an authentic list of pasteboard acquaintances to invite to the receptions? And what would become of us without Receptions? Everybody likes to give them. Everybody flocks to them with much alacrity. When society calls the roll, we all know the penalty of being left out. Is there any intellectual or physical pleasure equal to that of jamming so many people into a house that they can hardly move, and treating them to a Babel of noises in which no one can make herself heard without screaming? There is nothing like a reception in any uncivilized country. It is so exhilarating! When a dozen or a hundred people are gathered together in a room, they all begin to raise their voices and to shout like pool-sellers in the noble rivalry of "warious langwidges," rasping their throats into bronchitis in the bidding of the conversational ring. If they spoke low, or even in the ordinary tone, conversation would be possible. But then it would not be a reception, as we understand it. We cannot neglect anywhere any of the pleasures of our social life. We train for it in lower assemblies. Half a dozen women in a "call" are obliged to shout, just for practice, so that they can be heard by everybody in the neighborhood except themselves. Do not men do the same? If they do, it only shows that men also are capable of the higher civilization.

But does society—that is, the intercourse of congenial people—depend upon the elaborate system of exchanging calls with hundreds of people who are not congenial? Such thoughts will sometimes come by a winter fireside of rational-talking friends, or at a dinner-party not too large for talk without a telephone, or in the summer-time by the sea, or in the cottage in the hills, when the fever of social life has got down to a normal temperature. We fancy that sometimes people will give way to a real enjoyment of life and that human intercourse will throw off this artificial and wearisome parade, and that if women look back with pride, as they may, upon their personal achievements and labors, they will also regard them with astonishment. Women, we read every day, long for the rights and privileges of men, and the education and serious purpose in life of men. And yet, such is the sweet self-sacrifice of their nature, they voluntarily take on burdens which men have never assumed, and which they would speedily cast off if they had. What should we say of men if they consumed half their time in paying formal calls upon each other merely for the sake of paying calls, and were low-spirited if they did not receive as many cards as they had dealt out to society? Have they not the time? Have women more time? and if they have, why should they spend it in this Sisyphus task? Would the social machine go to pieces—the inquiry is made in good faith, and solely for information —if they made rational business for themselves to be attended to, or even if they gave the time now given to calls they hate to reading and study, and to making their household civilizing centres of intercourse and enjoyment, and paid visits from some other motive than "clearing off their list?" If all the artificial round of calls and cards should tumble down, what valuable thing would be lost out of anybody's life?

The question is too vast for the Drawer, but as an experiment in sociology it would like to see the system in abeyance for one season. If at the end of it there had not been just as much social enjoyment as before, and there were not fewer women than usual down with nervous prostration, it would agree to start at its own expense a new experiment, to wit, a kind of Social Clearing-House, in which all cards should be delivered and exchanged, and all social debts of this kind be balanced by experienced book-keepers, so that the reputation of everybody for propriety and conventionality should be just as good as it is now.

9

THE DINNER-TABLE TALK

MANY people suppose that it is the easiest thing in the world to dine if you can get plenty to eat. This error is the foundation of much social misery. The world that never dines, and fancies it has a grievance justifying anarchy on that account, does not know how much misery it escapes. A great deal has been written about the art of dining. From time to time geniuses have appeared who knew how to compose a dinner; indeed, the art of doing it can be learned, as well as the art of cooking and serving it. It is often possible, also, under extraordinarily favorable conditions, to select a company congenial and varied and harmonious enough to dine together successfully. The tact for getting the right people together is perhaps rarer than the art of composing the dinner. But it exists. And an elegant table with a handsome and brilliant company about it is a common conjunction in this country. Instructions are not wanting as to the shape of the table and the size of the party; it is universally admitted that the number must be small. The big dinner-parties which are commonly made to pay off social debts are generally of the sort that one would rather contribute to in money than in personal attendance. When the dinner is treated as a means of discharging obligations, it loses all character, and becomes one of the social inflictions. While there is nothing in social intercourse so agreeable and inspiring as a dinner of the right sort, society has invented no infliction equal to a large dinner that does not "go," as the phrase is. Why it does not go when the viands are good and the company is bright, is one of the acknowledged mysteries.

There need be no mystery about it. The social instinct and the social habit are wanting to a great many people of uncommon intelligence and cultivation

—that sort of flexibility or adaptability that makes agreeable society. But this even does not account for the failure of so many promising dinners. The secret of this failure always is that the conversation is not general. The sole object of the dinner is talk—at least in the United States, where "good eating" is pretty common, however it may be in England, whence come rumors occasionally of accomplished men who decline to be interrupted by the frivolity of talk upon the appearance of favorite dishes. And private talk at a table is not the sort that saves a dinner; however good it is, it always kills it. The chance of arrangement is that the people who would like to talk together are not neighbors; and if they are, they exhaust each other to weariness in an hour, at least of topics which can be talked about with the risk of being overheard. A duet to be agreeable must be to a certain extent confidential, and the dinner-table duet admits of little except generalities, and generalities between two have their limits of entertainment. Then there is the awful possibility that the neighbors at table may have nothing to say to each other; and in the best-selected company one may sit beside a stupid man—that is, stupid for the purpose of a *tête-à-tête*. But this is not the worst of it. No one can talk well without an audience; no one is stimulated to say bright things except by the attention and questioning and interest of other minds. There is little inspiration in side talk to one or two. Nobody ought to go to a dinner who is not a good listener, and, if possible, an intelligent one. To listen with a show of intelligence is a great accomplishment. It is not absolutely essential that there should be a great talker or a number of good talkers at a dinner if all are good listeners, and able to "chip in" a little to the general talk that springs up. For the success of the dinner does not necessarily depend upon the talk being brilliant, but it does depend upon its being general, upon keeping the ball rolling round the table; the old-fashioned game becomes flat when the balls all disappear into private pockets. There are dinners where the object seems to be to pocket all the balls as speedily as possible.

We have learned that that is not the best game ; the best game is when you not only depend on the carom, but in going to the cushion before you carom ; that is to say, including the whole table, and making things lively. The hostess succeeds who is able to excite this general play of all the forces at the table, even using the silent but not non-elastic material as cushions, if one may continue the figure.

Is not this, O brothers and sisters, an evil under the sun, this dinner as it is apt to be conducted? Think of the weary hours you have given to a rite that should be the highest social pleasure ! How often when a topic is started that promises well, and might come to something in a general exchange of wit and fancy, and · some one begins to speak on it, and speak very well, too, have you not had a lady at your side cut in and give you her views on it—views that might be amusing if thrown out into the discussion, but which are simply impertinent as an interruption ! How often when you have tried to get a " rise " out of somebody opposite have you not had your neighbor cut in across you with some private depressing observation to your next neighbor! Private talk at a dinner-table is like private chat at a parlor musical, only it is more fatal to the general enjoyment. There is a notion that the art of conversation, the ability to talk well, has gone out. That is a great mistake. Opportunity is all that is needed. There must be the inspiration of the clash of minds and the encouragement of good listening. In an evening round the fire, when couples begin to whisper or talk low to each other, it is time to put out the lights. Inspiring interest is gone. The most brilliant talker in the world is dumb. People whose idea of a dinner is private talk between seat-neighbors should limit the company to two. They have no right to spoil what can be the most agreeable social institution that civilization has evolved.

NATURALIZATION.

S it possible for a person to be entirely naturalized?—that is, to be denationalized, to cast off the prejudice and traditions of one country and take up those of another; to give up what may be called the instinctive tendencies of one race and take up those of another. It is easy enough to swear off allegiance to a sovereign or a government, and to take on in intention new political obligations, but to separate one's self from the sympathies into which he was born is quite another affair. One is likely to remain in the inmost recesses of his heart an alien, and as a final expression of his feeling to hoist the green flag, or the dragon, or the cross of St. George. Probably no other sentiment is so strong in a man as that of attachment to his own soil and people, a sub-sentiment always remaining, whatever new and unbreakable attachments he may form. One can be very proud of his adopted country, and brag for it, and fight for it; but lying deep in a man's nature is something, no doubt, that no oath nor material interest can change, and that is never naturalized. We see this experiment in America more than anywhere else, because here meet more different races than anywhere else with the serious intention of changing their nationality. And we have a notion that there is something in our atmosphere, or opportunities, or our government, that makes this change more natural and reasonable than it has been anywhere else in history. It is always a surprise to us when a born citizen of the United States changes his allegiance, but it seems a thing of course that a person of any other country should, by an oath, become a good American, and we expect that the act will work a sudden change in him equal to that wrought in a man by what used to be called a conviction of sin. We expect that he will not only come into our family, but that he will at once assume all its traditions and dislikes, that whatever may have been his institutions or his race quarrels, the moving influence of his life hereafter will be the "Spirit of '76."

What is this naturalization, however, but a sort of parable of human life? Are we not always trying to adjust ourselves to new relations, to get naturalized into a new family? Does one ever do it entirely? And how much of the lonesomeness of life comes from the failure to do it! It is a tremendous experiment, we all admit, to separate a person from his race, from his country, from his climate, and the habits of his part of the country, by marriage; it is only an experiment differing in degree to introduce him by marriage into a new circle of kinsfolk. Is he ever anything but a sort of tolerated, criticised, or admired alien? Does the time ever come when the distinction ceases between his family and hers? They say love is stronger than death. It may also be stronger than family—while it lasts; but was there ever a woman yet whose most ineradicable feeling was not the sentiment of family and blood, a sort of base-line in life upon which trouble and disaster always throw her back? Does she ever lose the instinct of it? We used to say in jest that a patriotic man was always willing to sacrifice his wife's relations in war; but his wife took a different view of it; and when it becomes a question of office, is it not the wife's relations who get them? To be sure, Ruth said, thy people shall be my people, and where thou goest I will go, and all that, and this beautiful sentiment has touched all time, and man has got the historic notion that he is the head of things. But is it true that a woman is ever really naturalized? Is it in her nature to be? Love will carry her a great way, and to far countries, and to many endurances, and her capacity of self-sacrifice is greater than man's; but would she ever be entirely happy torn from her kindred, transplanted from the associations and interlacings of her family life? Does there anything really take the place of that entire ease and confidence that one has in kin, or the inborn longing for their sympathy and society? There are two

theories about life, as about naturalization : one is that love is enough, that intention is enough ; the other is that the
whole circle of human relations and attachments is to be considered in a marriage, and that in the long-run the question of family is a preponderating one.
Does the gate of divorce open more fre-
quently from following the one theory
than the other? If we were to adopt the
notion that marriage is really a tremendous act of naturalization, of absolute surrender on one side or the other of the
deepest sentiments and hereditary tendencies, would there be so many hasty marriages—slip-knots tied by one justice to
be undone by another ? The Drawer did
not intend to start such a deep question
as this. Hosts of people are yearly naturalized in this country, not from any love
of its institutions, but because they can
more easily get a living here, and they
really surrender none of their hereditary
ideas, and it is only human nature that
marriages should be made with like purpose and like reservations. These reservations do not, however, make the best

citizens or the most happy marriages. Would it be any better if country lines were obliterated, and the great brotherhood of peoples were established, and there was no such thing as patriotism or family, and marriage were as free to make and unmake as some people think it should be? Very likely, if we could radically change human nature. But human nature is the most obstinate thing that the International Conventions have to deal with.

ART OF GOVERNING.

E was saying, when he awoke one morning, " I wish I were governor of a small island, and had nothing to do but to get up and govern." It was an observation quite worthy of him, and one of general application, for there are many men who find it very difficult to get a living on their own resources, to whom it would be comparatively easy to be a very fair sort of governor. Everybody who has no official position or routine duty on a salary knows that the most trying moment in the twenty-four hours is that in which he emerges from the oblivion of sleep and faces life. Everything perplexing tumbles in upon him, all the

possible vexations of the day rise up before him, and he is little less than a hero
if he gets up cheerful.

It is not to be wondered at that people
crave office, some salaried position, in order to escape the anxieties, the personal
responsibilities, of a single-handed struggle with the world. It must be much
easier to govern an island than to carry
on almost any retail business. When the
governor wakes in the morning he thinks
first of his salary; he has not the least
anxiety about his daily bread or the support of his family. His business is all
laid out for him; he has not to create it.
Business comes to him; he does not have
to drum for it. His day is agreeably, even
if sympathetically, occupied with the troubles of other people, and nothing is so
easy to bear as the troubles of other people. After he has had his breakfast, and
read over the "Constitution," he has nothing to do but to "govern" for a few hours,
that is, to decide about things on general
principles, and with little personal application, and perhaps about large concerns
which nobody knows anything about, and

which are much easier to dispose of than the perplexing details of private life. He has to vote several times a day ; for giving a decision is really casting a vote ; but that is much easier than to scratch around in all the anxieties of a retail business. Many men who would make very respectable Presidents of the United States could not successfully run a retail grocery store· The anxieties of the grocery would wear them out. For consider the varied ability that the grocery requires—the foresight about the markets, to take advantage of an eighth per cent. off or on here and there ; the vigilance required to keep a " full line " and not overstock, to dispose of goods before they spoil or the popular taste changes ; the suavity and integrity and duplicity and fairness and adaptability needed to get customers and keep them ; the power to bear the daily and hourly worry ; the courage to face the ever-present spectre of " failure," which is said to come upon ninety merchants in a hundred ; the tact needed to meet the whims and the complaints of patrons, and the difficulty of getting the patrons who grumble most to pay in order to satisfy the creditors. When the retail grocer wakens in the morning he feels that his business is not going to come to him spontaneously ; he thinks of his rivals, of his perilous stock, of his debts and delinquent customers. He has no " Constitution " to go by, nothing but his wits and energy to set against the world that day, and every day the struggle and the anxiety are the same. What a number of details he has to carry in his head (consider, for instance, how many different kinds of cheese there are, and how different people hate and love the same kind), and how keen must be his appreciation of the popular taste ! The complexities and annoyances of his business are excessive, and he cannot afford to make many mistakes ; if he does, he will lose his business, and when a man fails in business (honestly), he loses his nerve, and his career is ended. It is simply amazing, when you consider it, the amount of talent shown in what are called the ordinary businesses of life.

It has been often remarked with how little wisdom the world is governed. That is the reason it is so easy to govern. "Uneasy lies the head that wears a crown" does not refer to the discomfort of wearing it, but to the danger of losing it, and of being put back upon one's native resources, having to run a grocery or to keep school. Nobody is in such a pitiable plight as a monarch or politician out of business. It is very difficult for either to get a living. A man who has once enjoyed the blessed feeling of awaking every morning with the thought that he has a certain salary despises the idea of having to drum up a business by his own talents. It does not disturb the waking hour at all to think that a deputation is waiting in the next room about a post-office in Indiana or about the codfish in Newfoundland waters—the man can take a second nap on any such affair; but if he knows that the living of himself and family that day depends upon his activity and intelligence, uneasy lies his head. There is something so restful and easy about public business! It is so simple! Take the average Congressman. The Secretary of the Treasury sends in an elaborate report

—a budget, in fact—involving a complete and harmonious scheme of revenue and expenditure. Must the Congressman read it? No; it is not necessary to do that; he only cares for practical measures. Or a financial bill is brought in. Does he study that bill? He hears it read, at least by title. Does he take pains to inform himself by reading and conversation with experts upon its probable effect? Or an international copyright law is proposed, a measure that will relieve the people of the United States from the world-wide reputation of sneaking meanness towards foreign authors. Does he examine the subject, and try to understand it? That is not necessary. Or it is a question of tariff. He is to vote "yes" or "no" on these proposals. It is not necessary for him to master these subjects, but it is necessary for him to know how to vote. And how does he find out that? In the first place, by inquiring what effect the measure will have upon the chance of election of the man he thinks will be nominated for President, and in the second place, what effect his vote will have on his own re-election.

Thus the principles of legislation become very much simplified, and thus it happens that it is comparatively so much easier to govern than it is to run a grocery store.

LOVE OF DISPLAY.

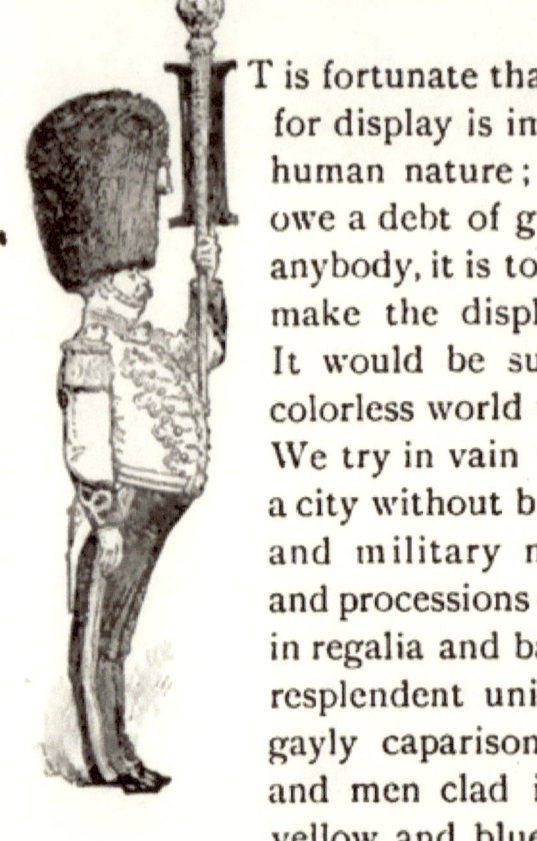

T is fortunate that a passion for display is implanted in human nature; and if we owe a debt of gratitude to anybody, it is to those who make the display for us. It would be such a dull, colorless world without it! We try in vain to imagine a city without brass bands, and military marchings, and processions of societies in regalia and banners and resplendent uniforms, and gayly caparisoned horses, and men clad in red and yellow and blue and gray and gold and silver and feathers, moving in beautiful lines, proudly wheeling with step elate upon some responsive human being as axis, deploying, opening, and closing ranks in exquisite precision to the strains of martial music, to the thump of the drum and the scream of the fife,

going away down the street with nodding
plumes, heads erect, the very port of heroism. There is scarcely anything in the
world so inspiring as that. And the self-
sacrifice of it! What will not men do
and endure to gratify their fellows! And
in the heat of summer, too, when most
we need something to cheer us! The
Drawer saw, with feelings that cannot be
explained, a noble company of men, the
pride of their city, all large men, all fat
men, all dressed alike, but each one as
beautiful as anything that can be seen on
the stage, perspiring through the gala
streets of another distant city, the admiration of crowds of huzzaing men and
women and boys, following another company as resplendent as itself, every man
bearing himself like a hero, despising the
heat and the dust, conscious only of doing his duty. We make a great mistake
if we suppose it is a feeling of ferocity
that sets these men tramping about in
gorgeous uniform, in mud or dust, in rain
or under a broiling sun. They have no
desire to kill anybody. Out of these resplendent clothes they are much like other

people; only they have a nobler spirit, that which leads them to endure hardships for the sake of pleasing others. They differ in degree, though not in kind, from those orders, for keeping secrets, or for encouraging a distaste for strong drink, which also wear bright and attractive regalia, and go about in processions, with banners and music, and a pomp that cannot be distinguished at a distance from real war. It is very fortunate that men do like to march about in ranks and lines, even without any distinguishing apparel. The Drawer has seen hundreds of citizens in a body, going about the country on an excursion, parading through town after town, with no other distinction of dress than a uniform high white hat, who carried joy and delight wherever they went. The good of this display cannot be reckoned in figures. Even a funeral is comparatively dull without the military band and the four-and-four processions, and the cities where these resplendent corteges of woe are of daily occurrence are cheerful cities. The brass band itself, when we consider it philosophically, is one of the most striking things in our civilization. We admire its commonly splendid clothes, its drums and cymbals and braying brass, but it is the impartial spirit with which it lends itself to our varying wants that distinguishes it. It will not do to say that it has no principles, for nobody has so many, or is so impartial in exercising them. It is equally ready to play at a festival or a funeral, a picnic or an encampment, for the sons of war or the sons of temperance, and it is equally willing to express the feeling of a Democratic meeting or a Republican gathering, and impartially blows out "Dixie" or "Marching through Georgia," "The Girl I Left Behind Me" or "My Country, 'tis of Thee." It is equally piercing and exciting for St. Patrick or the Fourth of July.

There are cynics who think it strange that men are willing to dress up in fantastic uniform and regalia and march about in sun and rain to make a holiday for their countrymen, but the cynics are ungrateful, and fail to credit human nature with its trait of self-sacrifice, and they do not at all comprehend our civilization. It was doubted at one time whether the freedman and the colored man generally in the republic was capable of the higher civilization. This doubt has all been removed. No other race takes more kindly to martial and civic display than it. No one has a greater passion for societies and uniforms and regalias and banners, and the pomp of marchings and processions and peaceful war. The negro naturally inclines to the picturesque, to the flamboyant, to vivid colors and the trappings of office that give a man distinction. He delights in the drum and the trumpet, and so willing is he to add to what is spectacular and pleasing in life that he would spend half his time in parading. His capacity for a holiday is practically unlimited. He has not yet the means to indulge his taste, and perhaps his taste is not yet equal to his means, but there is no question of his adaptability to the sort of display which is so pleasing to the greater part of the human race, and which contributes so much to the brightness and cheerfulness of this world.

We cannot all have decorations, and cannot all wear uniforms, or even regalia, and some of us have little time for going about in military or civic processions, but we all like to have our streets put on a holiday appearance; and we cannot express in words our gratitude to those who so cheerfully spend their time and money in glittering apparel and in parades for our entertainment.

VALUE OF THE COMMONPLACE.

THE vitality of a fallacy is incalculable. Although the Drawer has been going many years, there are still remaining people who believe that "things which are equal to the same thing are equal to each other." This mathematical axiom, which is well enough in its place, has been extended into the field of morals and social life, confused the perception of human relations, and raised "hob," as the saying is, in political economy. We theorize and legislate as if people were things. Most of the schemes of social reorganization are based on this fallacy. It always breaks down in experience. A has two friends, B and C — to state it mathematically. A is equal to B, and A is equal to C. A has for B and also for C the most cordial admiration and affection, and B and C have reciprocally the same feeling for

A. Such is the harmony that A cannot tell which he is more fond of, B or C. And B and C are sure that A is the best friend of each. This harmony, however, is not triangular. A makes the mistake of supposing that it is—having a notion that things which are equal to the same thing are equal to each other—and he brings B and C together. The result is disastrous. B and C cannot get on with each other. Regard for A restrains their animosity, and they hypocritically pretend to like each other, but both wonder what A finds so congenial in the other. The truth is that this personal equation, as we call it, in each cannot be made the subject of mathematical calculation. Human relations will not bend to it. And yet we keep blundering along as if they would. We are always sure, in our letter of introduction, that this friend will be congenial to the other, because we are fond of both. Sometimes this happens, but half the time we should be more successful in bringing people into accord if we gave a letter of introduction to a person we do not know, to be delivered to one we have never seen. On the face of it this is as absurd as it is for a politician to indorse the application of a person he does not know for an office the duties of which he is unacquainted with; but it is scarcely less absurd than the expectation that men and women can be treated like mathematical units and equivalents. Upon the theory that they can, rest the present grotesque schemes of Nationalism.

In saying all this the Drawer is well aware that it subjects itself to the charge of being commonplace, but it is precisely the commonplace that this essay seeks to defend. Great is the power of the commonplace. "My friends," says the preacher, in an impressive manner, "Alexander died; Napoleon died; you will all die!" This profound remark, so true, so thoughtful, creates a deep sensation. It is deepened by the statement that "man is a moral being." The profundity of such startling assertions cows the spirit; they appeal to the universal consciousness, and we bow to the genius that delivers them. "How true!" we exclaim, and go away with an enlarged sense of our own capacity for the comprehension of deep thought. Our conceit is flattered. Do we not like the books that raise us to the great level of the commonplace, whereon we move with a sense of power? Did not Mr. Tupper, that sweet, melodious shepherd of the undisputed, lead about vast flocks of sheep over the satisfying plain of mediocrity? Was there ever a greater exhibition of power, while it lasted? How long did "The Country Parson" feed an eager world with rhetorical statements of that which it already knew? The thinner this sort of thing is spread out, the more surface it covers, of course. What is so captivating and popular as a book of essays which gathers together and arranges a lot of facts out of histories and cyclopædias, set forth in the form of conversations that any one could have taken part in? Is not this book pleasing because it is commonplace? And is this because we do not like to be insulted with originality, or because in our experience it is only the commonly accepted which is true? The statesman

or the poet who launches out unmindful
of these conditions will be likely to come
to grief in his generation. Will not the
wise novelist seek to encounter the least
intellectual resistance?

Should one take a cynical view of man-
kind because he perceives this great power
of the commonplace? Not at all. He
should recognize and respect this power.
He may even say that it is this power
that makes the world go on as smoothly
and contentedly as it does, on the whole.
Woe to us, is the thought of Carlyle, when
a thinker is let loose in this world! He
becomes a cause of uneasiness, and a
source of rage very often. But his power
is limited. He filters through a few
minds, until gradually his ideas become
commonplace enough to be powerful.
We draw our supply of water from reser-
voirs, not from torrents. Probably the
man who first said that the line of recti-
tude corresponds with the line of enjoyment was disliked as well as disbelieved.
But how impressive now is the idea that
virtue and happiness are twins!

Perhaps it is true that the commonplace needs no defence, since everybody takes it in as naturally as milk, and thrives on it. Beloved and read and followed is the writer or the preacher of common-place. But is not the sunshine common, and the bloom of May? Why struggle with these things in literature and in life? Why not settle down upon the formula that to be platitudinous is to be happy?

THE BURDEN OF CHRISTMAS.

IT would be the pity of the world to destroy it, because it would be next to impossible to make another holiday as good as Christmas. Perhaps there is no danger, but the American people have developed an unexpected capacity for destroying things; they can destroy anything. They have even invented a phrase for it—running a thing into the ground. They have perfected the art of making so much of a thing as to kill it; they can magnify a man or a recreation or an institution to death. And they do it with such a hearty good-will and enjoyment. Their motto is that you cannot have too much of a good thing. They have almost made funerals unpopular by over-elaboration and display, especially what are called public funerals, in which an effort is made to confer great distinction on the dead. So far has it been carried often that there has been a reaction of popular sentiment and people have wished the man were alive. We prosecute everything so vigorously that we speedily either wear it out or wear ourselves out on it, whether it is a game, or a festival, or a holiday. We can use up any sport or game ever invented quicker than any other people. We can practise anything, like a vegetable diet, for instance, to an absurd conclusion with more vim than any other nation. This trait has its advantages; nowhere else will a delusion run so fast, and so soon run up a tree—another of our happy phrases. There is a largeness and exuberance about us which run even into our ordinary phraseology. The sympathetic clergyman, coming from the bedside of a parishioner dying of dropsy, says, with a heavy sigh, "The poor fellow is just swelling away."

Is Christmas swelling away? If it is not, it is scarcely our fault. Since the Ameri-

can nation fairly got hold of the holiday
—in some parts of the country, as in New
England, it has been universal only about
fifty years—we have made it hum, as we
like to say. We have appropriated the
English conviviality, the German simplicity, the Roman pomp, and we have added
to it an element of expense in keeping with
our own greatness. Is anybody beginning
to feel it a burden, this sweet festival of
charity and good-will, and to look forward
to it with apprehension? Is the time approaching when we shall want to get
somebody to play it for us, like base-ball?
Anything that interrupts the ordinary
flow of life, introduces into it, in short, a
social cyclone that upsets everything for
a fortnight, may in time be as hard to bear
as that festival of housewives called house-
cleaning, that riot of cleanliness which
men fear as they do a panic in business.
Taking into account the present prepara-
tions for Christmas, and the time it takes
to recover from it, we are beginning—are
we not?—to consider it one of the most
serious events of modern life.

The Drawer is led into these observations out of its love for Christmas. It is impossible to conceive of any holiday that could take its place, nor indeed would it seem that human wit could invent another so adapted to humanity. The obvious intention of it is to bring together, for a season at least, all men in the exercise of a common charity and a feeling of goodwill, the poor and the rich, the successful and the unfortunate, that all the world may feel that in the time called the Truce of God the thing common to all men is the best thing in life. How will it suit this intention, then, if in our way of exaggerated ostentation of charity the distinction between rich and poor is made to appear more marked than on ordinary days? Blessed are those that expect nothing. But are there not an increasing multitude of persons in the United States who have the most exaggerated expectations of personal profit on Christmas Day? Perhaps it is not quite so bad as this, but it is safe to say that what the children alone expect to receive, in money value would absorb the national surplus, about which so much fuss is made. There is really no objection to this—the terror of the surplus is a sort of nightmare in the country—except that it destroys the simplicity of the festival, and belittles small offerings that have their chief value in affection. And it points inevitably to the creation of a sort of Christmas "Trust"—the modern escape out of ruinous competition. When the expense of our annual charity becomes so great that the poor are discouraged from sharing in it, and the rich even feel it a burden, there would seem to be no way but the establishment of neighborhood "Trusts" in order to equalize both cost and distribution. Each family could buy a share according to its means, and the division on Christmas Day would create a universal satisfaction in profit sharing—that is, the rich would get as much as the poor, and the rivalry of ostentation would be quieted. Perhaps with the money question a little subdued, and the female anxieties of the festival allayed, there would be more room for the development of that sweet spirit of brotherly kindness, or all-embracing charity, which we know underlies this best festival

of all the ages.   Is this an old sermon?
The Drawer trusts that it is, for there can
be nothing new in the preaching of simplicity.

THE RESPONSIBILITY OF WRITERS.

IT is difficult enough to keep the world straight without the interposition of fiction. But the conduct of the novelists and the painters makes the task of the conservators of society doubly perplexing. Neither the writers nor the artists have a due sense of the responsibilities of their creations. The trouble appears to arise from the imitativeness of the race. Nature herself seems readily to fall into imitation. It was noticed by the friends of nature that when the peculiar coal-tar colors were discovered, the same faded, æsthetic, and sometimes sickly colors began to appear in the ornamental flower-beds and masses of foliage plants. It was hardly fancy that the flowers took the colors of the ribbons and stuffs of the looms, and that the same instant nature and art were sicklied o'er with the same pale hues of fashion.

If this relation of nature and art is too subtle for comprehension, there is nothing fanciful in the influence of the characters in fiction upon social manners and morals. To convince ourselves of this, we do not need to recall the effect of Werther, of Childe Harold, and of Don Juan, and the imitation of their sentimentality, misanthropy, and adventure, down to the copying of the rakishness of the loosely - knotted necktie and the broad turn-over collar. In our own generation the heroes and heroines of fiction begin to appear in real life, in dress and manner, while they are still warm from the press. The popular heroine appears on the street in a hundred imitations as soon as the popular mind apprehends her traits in the story. We did not know the type of woman in the poems of the æsthetic school and on the canvas of Rossetti—the red-haired, wide-eyed child of passion and emotion, in lank clothes, enmeshed in spider-webs—but so quickly was she multiplied in real life that she seemed to have stepped from the book and the frame, ready-made, into the street and the drawing-room. And there is nothing wonderful about this. It is a truism to say that the genuine creations in fiction take their places in general apprehension with historical characters, and sometimes they live more vividly on the printed page and on canvas than the others in their pale, contradictory, and incomplete lives. The characters of history we seldom agree about, and are always reconstructing on new information; but the characters of fiction are subject to no such vicissitudes.

The importance of this matter is hardly yet perceived. Indeed, it is unreasonable that it should be, when parents, as a rule, have so slight a feeling of responsibility for the sort of children they bring into the world. In the coming scientific age this may be changed, and society may visit upon a grandmother the sins of her grandchildren, recognizing her responsibility to the very end of the line. But it is not strange that in the apathy on this subject the novelists should be careless and inconsiderate as to the characters they produce, either as ideals or examples. They know that the bad example is more likely to be copied than to be shunned, and that the low ideal, being easy to follow, is more likely to be imitated than the high ideal. But the novelists have too little sense of responsibility in this respect, probably from an inadequate conception of their power. Perhaps the most harmful sinners are not those who send into the world of fiction the positively wicked and immoral, but those who make current the dull, the commonplace, and the socially vulgar. For most readers the wicked character is repellent; but the commonplace raises less protest, and is soon deemed harmless, while it is most demoralizing. An underbred book—that is, a book in which the underbred characters are the natural outcome of the author's own mind and apprehension of life—is worse than any possible epidemic ; for while the epidemic may kill a number of useless or vulgar people, the book will make a great number. The keen observer must have noticed the increasing number of commonplace, undiscriminating people of low intellectual taste in the United States. These are to a degree the result of the feeble, underbred literature (so called) that is most hawked about, and most accessib'e, by cost and exposure, to the greater number of people. It is easy to distinguish the young ladies — many of them beautifully dressed, and handsome on first acquaintance — who have been bred on this kind of book. They are betrayed by their speech, their taste, their manners. Yet there is a marked public insensibility about this. We all admit that the scrawny young woman, anæmic and physically undeveloped, has not had proper nourishing food. But we seldom think that the mentally-vulgar girl, poverty-stricken in ideas, has been starved by a thin course of diet on anæmic books. The girls are not to blame if they are as vapid and uninteresting as the ideal girls they have been associating with in the books they have read. The responsibility is with the novelist and the writer of stories, the chief characteristic of which is vulgar commonplace.

Probably when the Great Assize is held one of the questions asked will be, " Did you, in America, ever write stories for children?" What a quaking of knees there will be! For there will stand the victims of this sort of literature, who began in their tender years to enfeeble their minds with the wishy-washy flood of commonplace prepared for them by dull writers and commercial publishers, and continued on in those so-called domestic stories (as if domestic meant idiotic) until their minds were diluted to that degree that they could not act upon anything that offered the least resistance. Beginning with the pepsinized books, they must continue with them, and the dull appetite by-and-by must be stimulated with a spice of vulgarity or a little pepper of impropriety. And fortunately for their nourishment in this kind, the dullest writers can be indecent.

Unfortunately the world is so ordered that the person of the feeblest constitution can communicate a contagious disease. And these people, bred on this pabulum, in turn make books. If one, it is now admitted, can do nothing else in this world, he can write, and so the evil widens and widens. No art is required, nor any selection, nor any ideality, only capacity for increasing the vacuous commonplace in life. A princess born may have this, or the leader of cotillons. Yet in the Judgment the responsibility will rest upon the writers who set the copy.

THE CAP AND GOWN.

ONE of the burning questions now in the colleges for the higher education of women is whether the undergraduates shall wear the cap and gown. The subject is a delicate one, and should not be confused with the broader one, what is the purpose of the higher education? Some hold that the purpose is to enable a woman to dispense with

13

marriage, while others maintain that it is to fit a woman for the higher duties of the married life. The latter opinion will probably prevail, for it has nature on its side, and the course of history, and the imagination. But meantime the point of education is conceded, and whether a girl is to educate herself into single or double blessedness need not interfere with the consideration of the habit she is to wear during her college life. That is to be determined by weighing a variety of reasons.

Not the least of these is the consideration whether the cap-and-gown habit is becoming. If it is not becoming, it will not go, not even by an amendment to the Constitution of the United States; for woman's dress obeys always the higher law. Masculine opinion is of no value on this point, and the Drawer is aware of the fact that if it thinks the cap and gown becoming, it may imperil the cap-and-gown cause to say so; but the cold truth is that the habit gives a plain girl distinction, and a handsome girl gives the habit distinction. So that, aside from the mysterious working of feminine motive, which makes woman a law unto herself, there should be practical unanimity in regard to this habit. There is in the cap and gown a subtle suggestion of the union of learning with womanly charm that is very captivating to the imagination. On the other hand, all this may go for nothing with the girl herself, who is conscious of the possession of quite other powers and attractions in a varied and constantly changing toilet, which can reflect her moods from hour to hour. So that if it is admitted that this habit is almost universally becoming to-day, it might, in the inscrutable depths of the feminine nature—the something that education never can and never should change—be irksome to-morrow, and we can hardly imagine what a blight to a young spirit there might be in three hundred and sixty-five days of uniformity.

The devotees of the higher education will perhaps need to approach the subject from another point of view—namely, what they are willing to surrender in order to come into a distinctly scholastic influence. The cap and gown are scholastic emblems. Primarily they marked the student, and not alliance with any creed or vows to any religious order. They belong to the universities of learning, and to-day they have no more ecclesiastic meaning than do the gorgeous robes of the Oxford chancellor and vice-chancellor and the scarlet hood. From the scholarly side, then, if not from the dress side, there is much to be said for the cap and gown. They are badges of devotion, for the time being, to an intellectual life. They help the mind in its effort to set itself apart to unworldly pursuits; they are indications of separateness from the prevailing fashions and frivolities. The girl who puts on the cap and gown devotes herself to the society which is avowedly in pursuit of a larger intellectual sympathy and a wider intellectual life. The enduring of this habit will have a confirming influence on her purposes, and help to keep her up to them. It is like the uniform to the soldier or the veil to the nun—a sign of separation and devotion. It is difficult in this age to keep any historic consciousness, any proper relations to the past. In the cap and gown the girl will at least feel that she is in the line of the traditions of pure learning. And there is also something of order and discipline in the uniforming of a community set apart for an unworldly purpose. Is it believed that three or four years of the kind of separateness marked by this habit in the life of a girl will rob her of any desirable womanly quality?

The cap and gown are only an emphasis of the purpose to devote a certain period to the higher life, and if they cannot be defended, then we may begin to be sceptical about the seriousness of the intention of a higher education. If the school is merely a method of passing the time until a certain event in the girl's life, she had better dress as if that event were the only one worth considering. But if she wishes to fit herself for the best married life, she may not disdain the help of the cap and gown in devoting herself to the highest culture. Of course education has its dangers, and the regalia of scholarship may increase them. While our cap-and-gown divinity is walking in the groves of Academia, apart from the ways of men, her sisters outside may be dancing and dressing into the affections of the marriageable men. But this is not the worst of it. The university girl may be educating herself out of sympathy with the ordinary possible husband. But this will carry its own cure. The educated girl will be so much more attractive in the long-run, will have so many more resources for making a life companionship agreeable, that she will be more and more in demand. And the young men, even those not expecting to take up a learned profession, will see the advantage of educating themselves up to the cap-and-gown level. We know that it is the office of the university to raise the standard of the college, and of the college to raise the standard of the high school. It will be the inevitable result that these young ladies, setting themselves apart for a period to the intellectual life, will raise the standard of the young men, and of married life generally. And there is nothing supercilious in the invitation of the cap-and-gown brigade to the young men to come up higher.

There is one humiliating objection made to the cap and gown — made by members of the gentle sex themselves — which cannot be passed by. It is of such a delicate nature, and involves such a disparagement of the sex in a vital point, that the Drawer hesitates to put it in words. It is said that the cap and gown will be used to cover untidiness, to conceal the makeshift of a disorderly and unsightly toilet. Undoubtedly the cap and gown are democratic, adopted probably to equalize the appearance of rich and poor in the same institution, where all are on an intellectual level. Perhaps the sex is not perfect; it may be that there are slovens (it is a brutal word) in that sex which is our poetic image of purity. But a neat and self-respecting girl will no more be slovenly under a scholastic gown than under any outward finery. If it is true that the sex would take cover in this way, and is liable to run down at the heel when it has a chance, then to the "examination" will have to be added a periodic "inspection," such as the West-Pointers submit to in regard to their uniforms. For the real idea of the cap and gown is to encourage discipline, order, and neatness. We fancy that it is the mission of woman in this generation to show the world that the tendency of women to an intellectual life is not, as it used to be said it was, to untidy habits.

A TENDENCY OF THE AGE.

THIS ingenious age, when studied, seems not less remarkable for its division of labor than for the disposition of people to shift labor on to other's shoulders. Perhaps it is only another aspect of the spirit of altruism, a sort of backhanded vicariousness. In taking an inventory of tendencies, this demands some attention.

The notion appears to be spreading that there must be some way by which one can get a good intellectual outfit without much personal effort. There are many schemes of education which encourage this idea. If one could only hit upon the right "electives," he could become a scholar with very little study, and without grappling with any of the real difficulties in the way of an education. It is not more a short-cut we desire, but a road of easy grades, with a locomotive that will pull our train along while we sit in a palace-car at ease. The discipline to be obtained by tackling an obstacle and overcoming it we think of small value. There must be some way of attaining the end of cultivation without much labor. We take readily to proprietary medicines. It is easier to dose with these than to exercise ordinary prudence about our health. And we readily believe the doctors of learning when they assure us that we can acquire a new language by the same method by which we can restore bodily vigor : take one small patent-right volume in six easy lessons, without even the necessity of "shaking," and without a regular doctor, and we shall know the language. Some one else has done all the work for us, and we only need to absorb. It is pleasing to see how this theory is getting to be universally applied. All knowledge can be put into a kind of pemican, so that we can have it condensed. Everything must be chopped up, epitomized, put in short sentences, and italicized. And we have primers for science, for history, so that we can acquire all the information we need in this world in a few hasty bites. It is an admirable saving of time — saving of time being more important in this generation than the saving of ourselves.

And the age is so intellectually active, so eager to know! If we wish to know anything, instead of digging for it ourselves, it is much easier to flock all together to some lecturer who has put all the results into an hour, and perhaps can throw them all upon a screen, so that we can acquire all we want by merely using the eyes, and bothering ourselves little about what is said. Reading itself is almost too much of an effort. We hire people to read for us—to interpret, as we call it—Browning and Ibsen, even Wagner. Every one is familiar with the pleasure and profit of "recitations," of "conversations" which are monologues. There is something fascinating in the scheme of getting others to do our intellectual labor for us, to attempt to fill up our minds as if they were jars. The need of the mind for nutriment is like the need of the body, but our theory is that it can be satisfied in a different way. There was an old belief that in order that we should enjoy food, and that it should perform its function of assimilation, we must work for it, and that the exertion needed to earn it brought the appetite that made it profitable to the system. We still have the idea that we must eat for ourselves, and that we cannot delegate this performance, as we do the filling of the mind, to some one else. We may have ceased to relish the act of eating, as we have ceased to relish the act of studying, but we cannot yet delegate it, even although our power of digesting food for the body has become almost as feeble as the power of acquiring and digesting food for the mind.

It is beautiful to witness our reliance upon others. The house may be full of books, the libraries may be as free and as unstrained of impurities as city water; but if we wish to read anything or study anything we resort to a club. We gather together a number of persons of like capacity with ourselves. A subject which we might grapple with and run down by a few hours of vigorous, absorbed attention in a library, gaining strength of mind by resolute encountering of difficulties, by personal effort, we sit around for a month or a season in a club, expecting somehow to take the information by effortless contiguity with it. A book which we could master and possess in an evening we can have read to us in a month in the club, without the least intellectual effort. Is there nothing, then, in the exchange of ideas? Oh yes, when there are ideas to exchange. Is there nothing stimulating in the conflict of mind with mind? Oh yes, when there is any mind for a conflict. But the mind does not grow without personal effort and conflict and struggle with itself. It is a living organism, and not at all like a jar or other receptacle for fluids. The physiologists say that what we eat will not do us much good unless we chew it. By analogy we may presume that the mind is not greatly benefited by what it gets without considerable exercise of the mind.

Still, it is a beautiful theory that we can get others to do our reading and thinking, and stuff our minds for us. It may be that psychology will yet show us how a congregate education by clubs may be the way. But just now the method is a little crude, and lays us open to the charge—which every intelligent person of this scientific age will repudiate—of being content with the superficial; for instance, of trusting wholly to others for our immortal furnishing, as many are satisfied with the review of a book for the book itself, or—a refinement on that—with a review of the reviews. The method is still crude. Perhaps we may expect a further development of the "slot" machine. By dropping a cent in the slot one can get his weight, his age, a piece of chewing-gum, a bit of candy, or a shock that will energize his nervous system. Why not get from a similar machine a "good business education," or an "interpretation" of Browning, or a new language, or a knowledge of English literature? But even this would be crude. We have hopes of something from electricity. There ought to be somewhere a reservoir of knowledge, connected by wires with every house, and a professional switch-tender, who, upon the pressure of a button in any house, could turn on the intellectual stream desired. There must be discovered in time a method by which not only information but intellectual life can be infused into the system by an electric current. It would save a world of trouble and expense. For some clubs even are a weariness, and it costs money to hire other people to read and think for us.

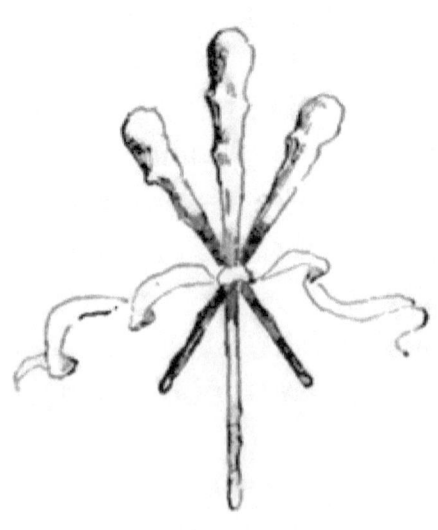

THE
CENSUS.
—

A LOCOED
NOVELIST.

Either we have been indulging in an expensive mistake, or a great foreign novelist who preaches the gospel of despair is *locoed*.

This word, which may be new to most of our readers, has long been current in the Far West, and is likely to be adopted into the language, and become as indispensable as the typic words *taboo* and *tabooed*, which Herman Melville gave us some forty years ago. . There grows upon the deserts and the cattle ranges of the Rockies a slender plant of the lobelia family, with a purple blossom, which is called the *loco*. It is sweet to the taste ; horses and cattle are fond of it, and when they have once eaten it they prefer it to anything else, and often refuse other food. But the plant is poisonous, or, rather, to speak exactly, it is a weed of insanity. Its effect upon the horse seems to be mental quite as much as physical. He behaves queerly, he is full of whims ; one would say he was " possessed." He takes freaks, he trembles, he will not go in certain places, he will not pull straight, his mind is evidently affected, he is mildly insane. In point of fact, he is ruined ; that is to say, he is *locoed*. Further indulgence in the plant results in death, but rarely does an animal recover from even one eating of the insane weed.

The shepherd on the great sheep ranges leads an absolutely isolated life. For weeks, sometimes for months together, he does not see a human being. His only companions are his dogs and the three or four thousand sheep he is herding. All

day long, under the burning sun, he fol-
lows the herd over the rainless prairie, as
it nibbles here and there the short grass
and slowly gathers its food. At night he
drives the sheep back to the corral, and
lies down alone in his hut. He speaks to
no one; he almost forgets how to speak.
Day and night he hears no sound except
the melancholy, monotonous bleat, bleat
of the sheep. It becomes intolerable.
The animal stupidity of the herd enters
into him. Gradually he loses his mind.
They say that he is *locoed*. The insane
asylums of California contain many shep-
herds.

But the word *locoed* has come to have
a wider application than to the poor shep-
herds or the horses and cattle that have
eaten the *loco*. Any one who acts queerly,
talks strangely, is visionary without being
actually a lunatic, who is what would be
called elsewhere a "crank," is said to be
locoed. It is a term describing a shade of
mental obliquity and queerness something
short of irresponsible madness, and something more than temporarily "rattled" or
bewildered for the moment. It is a good

word, and needed to apply to many people who have gone off into strange ways, and behave as if they had eaten some insane plant—the insane plant being probably a theory in the mazes of which they have wandered until they are lost.

Perhaps the *loco* does not grow in Russia, and the Prophet of Discouragement may never have eaten of it ; perhaps he is only like the shepherd, mainly withdrawn from human intercourse and sympathy in a morbid mental isolation, hearing only the bleat, bleat, bleat of the *muzhiks* in the dulness of the steppes, wandering round in his own sated mind until he has lost all clew to life. Whatever the cause may be, clearly he is *locoed*. All his theories have worked out to the conclusion that the world is a gigantic mistake, love is nothing but animality, marriage is immorality ; according to astronomical calculations this teeming globe and all its life must end some time ; and why not now ? There shall be no more marriage, no more children ; the present population shall wind up its affairs with decent haste, and one by one quit the scene of their failure, and avoid all the worry of a useless struggle.

This gospel of the blessedness of extinction has come too late to enable us to profit by it in our decennial enumeration. How different the census would have been if taken in the spirit of this new light ! How much bitterness, how much hateful rivalry would have been spared ! We should then have desired a reduction of the population, not an increase of it. There would have been a pious rivalry among all the towns and cities on the way to the millennium of extinction to show the least number of inhabitants ; and those towns would have been happiest which could exhibit not only a marked decline in numbers, but the greater number of old people. Beautiful St. Paul would have held a thanksgiving service, and invited the Minneapolis enumerators to the feast. Kansas City and St. Louis and San Francisco, and a hundred other places, would not have desired a recount, except, perhaps, for overestimate ; they would not have said that thousands were away at the sea or in the mountains, but, on the contrary, that thousands who did not belong there, attracted by the salubrity of the climate, and the desire to injure the town's reputation, had crowded in there in census time. The newspapers, instead of calling on people to send in the names of the unenumerated, would have rejoiced at the small returns, as they would have done if the census had been for the purpose of levying the federal tax upon each place according to its population. Chicago—well, perhaps the Prophet of the Steppes would have made an exception of Chicago, and been cynically delighted to push it on its way of increase, aggregation, and ruin.

But instead of this, the strain of anxiety was universal and heart-rending. So much depended upon swelling the figures. The tension would have been relieved if our faces were all set towards extinction, and the speedy evacuation of this unsatisfactory globe. The writer met recently, in the Colorado desert of Arizona, a forlorn census-taker who had been six weeks in the saddle, roaming over the alkali plains in order to gratify the vanity of Uncle Sam. He had lost his reckoning, and did not know the day of the week or of the month. In all the vast territory, away up to the Utah line, over which he had wandered, he met human beings (excluding " Indians and others not taxed") so rarely that he was in danger of being *lococd*. He was almost in despair when, two days before, he had a windfall, which raised his general average, in the form of a woman with twenty-six children, and he was rejoicing that he should be able to turn in one hundred and fifty people. Alas, the revenue the government will derive from these half-nomads will never pay the cost of enumerating them.

And, alas again, whatever good showing we may make, we shall wish it were larger; the more people we have the more we shall want. In this direction there is no end, any more than there is to life. If extinction, and not life and growth, is the better rule, what a costly mistake we have been making!

www.ingramcontent.com/pod-product-compliance
Lightning Source LLC
Chambersburg PA
CBHW030122030726
47498CB00007B/2504